Fear was never far from her mind.

Even today, when Beckett had taken her out of hiding for horseback riding.

She scoped out the pastureland. "Are you sure we should be out in the open like this?"

"You'll be fine."

She took his word. "This is exactly what I needed. Thank you."

He smiled. "You're welcome."

Had she been wrong about the sheriff?

"Beckett, I have to tell you. You're good at this protection thing." No one was braver, stronger, smarter. "People need you."

He leaned across his horse and searched her eyes. "What people, Aurora? Who needs me?"

As she fell into his gaze, the words echoed in her head. *I need you.*

Before she could utter them, she heard the unmistakable sound.

Gunfire!

Her horse reared up then shot forward, nearly knocking her from the saddle. Panic went through her as another gunshot echoed through the woods and splintered the tree she darted past.

"Beckett!" She tugged on the reins but her horse ran out of control. Straight to the ravine.

Jessica R. Patch lives in the mid-South, where she pens inspirational contemporary romance and romantic suspense novels. When she's not hunched over her laptop or going on adventurous trips with willing friends in the name of research, you can find her watching way too much Netflix with her family and collecting recipes to amazing dishes she'll probably never cook. To learn more about Jessica, please visit her at jessicarpatch.com.

Books by Jessica R. Patch

Love Inspired Suspense

FINAL VERDICT

JESSICA R. PATCH

HARLEQUIN® LOVE INSPIRED® SUSPENSE

Recycling programs
for this product may
not exist in your area.

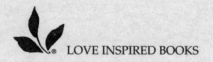

LOVE INSPIRED BOOKS

ISBN-13: 978-0-373-67820-4

Final Verdict

www.Harlequin.com

Printed in U.S.A.

My dear children, I am writing this to you so that you will not sin. But if anyone does sin, we have an advocate who pleads our case before the Father. He is Jesus Christ, the one who is truly righteous.

—1 John 2:1

To Chelsey Hale-Browning:
You are brave. You are strong. And I love you.

Many thanks go out to the following people:

My agent, Rachel Kent:
Thank you for being my champion.

My editor, Shana Asaro:
Thank you for deepening my stories
and pushing me to make them better.

My critique partners, Jill Kemerer and Susan Tuttle:
You girls consistently rescue this crazy writer!

To Assistant District Attorney Luke Williamson of Desoto
County, MS: You are my friend and a great plotter!
You should write a book.

To Deputy Chief Clint Taylor of Mt. Vernon, IL:
Thank you for all of your expertise
and patiently answering my questions.
Any mistakes in procedure are all mine.

To David Kolb:
Thank you for helping me with all things mechanic,
and for being a wonderful brother-in-law.
Anything I stretched is all on me!

ONE

Aurora Daniels inhaled the scent of justice wafting through the courtroom. Winning the motion would come at a grave price, no doubt. Every case she tried did. But her seventeen-year-old client, Austin Bledsoe, could be rehabilitated. It wasn't in the interest of justice to try the boy as an adult. To toss away the key on a kid who needed a champion, an advocate. A boy who reminded her remarkably of her older brother, Richie.

The courtroom had emptied several minutes ago, and she carefully placed her documents inside her briefcase, taking her time and hoping a mob wouldn't be waiting for her once she stepped foot into full-on February. Not nearly as frigid as Chicago temperatures, but Hope, Tennessee, could produce incredibly bitter wind and, occasionally, snow.

"Watch your back, Counselor."

Aurora plopped her phone into her coat pocket and whipped her head in the direction of the low but smooth male voice. Sheriff Beckett Marsh loomed at the doors to the courtroom, onyx eyebrows furrowing over intense eyes that matched his dark mood.

"You threatening me, Sheriff?" Beckett was honest and noble, but he was as fired up over the outcome of today's motion as the Russell family. Her heart pinched as she thought of them grieving in the right front row. But someone had to do this job. *She* had to.

"Warning." He uncrossed his right ankle from his left, pushed off the door frame and stalked her way, heavy work boots clunking on the freshly polished hardwood. He folded his muscular arms across his chest and Aurora worked to keep her wits. Beckett Marsh was ridiculously fit and attractive, but he wasn't a fan of hers professionally or—apparently—personally. Most law enforcers didn't care for defense attorneys. Especially those who were good at their profession. "You realize you've taken a murderer and allowed him to be slapped on the wrist."

Aurora raised her chin. "Austin Bledsoe has had no trouble with the law. He makes decent grades. His grandmother passed away two weeks ago. She was his only stability." Stability was everything she'd always wanted and never had, which was why she'd promised herself that, when she became an adult, she'd do whatever necessary to gain it. Enter accepting the position at Benard, Lowenstein & Meyer. What a nightmare that had turned out to be.

Beckett snorted. "So that makes drinking a bottle of Old Crow and gettin' drunker than Cooter Brown before plowing into a decent woman—on her way to church, no less—okay?"

"What he did was far from acceptable." Aurora's stomach knotted. "He made a fatal mistake in his grief, and he *will* face consequences—crushing guilt for the rest of his life, for one—but he won't be thrown away forever. He can be rehabilitated. I know it." Too bad she couldn't be rehabbed from her past shortcomings. No matter how many times her mentor promised her that God could free her from the guilt she carried, she couldn't muster enough faith to believe it.

"Well, Bethany Russell can't be."

Aurora dropped her head, torn between championing her client for a second chance and understanding the agonizing pain of the Russell family. She mourned her brother daily. They'd been close. If he could have hung on until she'd graduated law school and got ahold of those case files to exonerate him… But he had slipped away too soon. "I know that, too. Truth is no one won here today. No one."

"Guess we'll have to agree to disagree." Beckett ran his tongue along his full bottom lip. "In the meantime, you've got a big portion of the town in an uproar, and when you walk outside the courthouse it won't be the wind bitin' at your throat. It'll be grieving friends and family who expected a better outcome."

Aurora swallowed down a rush of anxiety. "Well…I appreciate the colorful depiction of my near future." She tried to slide by Beckett, but he grasped her forearm.

"Counselor, I cared about Bethany Russell and her family. And this town—this county. I'll do whatever I need to in order to protect the people who live here. My warning isn't to slice you. You're a citizen of Hope. I want you safe, so be careful." The edge in his eyes tempered a fraction and he released his civil grip.

"Thank you."

He jammed his hands into his coat pockets. "You want me to walk you to your car?"

She viewed the doors leading to the steps that would take her to her vehicle and to the throng of people who hated her for doing her job—for believing that everyone was entitled to a fair trial. They didn't understand that sometimes she disliked her clients more than anyone. Tossing her glance in Beckett's direction, she shook her head.

"I'm used to unkind words and threats, Sheriff. I've handled much worse." She still felt the stab anyway.

Beckett's eyebrows lifted. "You talking about losing Severin Renzetti's case in Chicago and angering a crime family two years ago?"

Aurora wasn't surprised the sheriff had done a background check on her. He was meticulous. Thorough. A former navy SEAL. The man who had a hand in taking down a major Mexican cartel back in June when his now good buddy, Holt McKnight, had come to town undercover for the DEA.

She wouldn't even be in his town of Hope if she hadn't been asked to resign over a stupid, overconfident slipup in the courtroom. She wouldn't be lying low here in hopes that Franco Renzetti, head of *the* largest crime family in Chicago, hadn't changed his mind and decided to seek further retribution for his son, Severin Renzetti's conviction. She thought of muttering a few prayers for safety, but passed. She didn't deserve them.

Aurora ignored Beckett's observation and opened the ornate wooden doors. The wintry gusts charged down her scarf and gray peacoat, forcing a shiver into her bones.

Squaring her shoulders, she met the crowd head-on and proceeded down the concrete steps, keeping her face masked from emotion. In Chicago, dozens of cameras had been thrust in front of her nose, reporters' voices toppling over each other as they begged for the scoop. Asking how it felt losing a case she had been confident of winning. Asking if the rumors of her and Severin Renzetti being romantically involved were true. They weren't. But the media skewed every detail.

Severin had been charming, though. He'd been charged and convicted of conspiracy to commit extortion and she had believed in his innocence, that he'd tried to come out from under his family's reputation to be a decent and honest man. Aurora had sympathized. She'd clawed her way out from under some heavy stereotypes herself. But, in the end, she'd been manipulated and preyed upon for trying to trust that there was good in everyone—or almost everyone—even the son of a mob boss.

"How could you do that, Miss Daniels? That boy killed Bethany Russell!" an older woman hollered.

A menacing voice carried over the woman's. "Better be careful on those roads, miss. Wouldn't want you to end up like Mrs. Russell."

Aurora darted her sight in the direction of the gritty voice. Didn't recognize it. Couldn't find the source. But the tone wasn't laced with grief like the others. No, this sounded ominous. She tugged her wool scarf tighter around her neck and picked up her pace, ignoring the snide comments on the outside. Inside, she had a more difficult time fielding the stings.

Glancing back one last time, she searched for the man who'd threatened her. She used the fob on her key ring, reached out to open the door to her BMW and cringed, then groaned at the long, keyed mark running the length of the driver's side. Had the man who'd threatened her keyed her car, too, or had that been the handiwork of someone else unhappy with her?

She spotted Beckett Marsh ambling toward her. Following and protecting her even if she had turned him down. "I can watch my back." She pointed to the deep gash ruining her shiny black paint. "My car not so much."

Beckett gave a low whistle as he rounded the car and stood beside her, blocking a frigid gust of winter with his body.

She tossed her handbag and briefcase inside as her cell phone rang.

Katelynn, her barista at Sufficient Grounds, was calling. She pulled the cell from her coat and answered. "Hi, Kate. What's going on?" Had her café been vandalized, too?

"The espresso machine is janky again. I've tried everything."

"You unplugged it, opened the back and jiggled the wires?"

"Jiggled, kicked…"

"Yes, because kicking a four-thousand-dollar machine is smart." Aurora would have done the same thing had she not known exactly which wires to tamper with. "Just—"

"Jiggle the wires again, I know. I did. You've got the touch." Katelynn's voice rose an octave. "Please. We've got a major crowd and they're all talking about the motion today. That you won. They aren't happy, but it appears they aren't mad enough to boycott the place."

"It's the little things." She'd leased the building and opened the coffeehouse when she'd moved to Hope to try to fit in. Working as the public defender didn't bring the best of friends. But coffee… Well, everyone liked coffee and camaraderie, and it had helped her acclimate. Until this.

Aurora eyed Beckett, who was in no hurry to leave or even pretend he wasn't listening to her conversation. "Be there in five." She hung up, slid into the driver's seat and turned the ignition on her car, then peered up at Beckett. "I've got to—"

"Jiggle wires." His lips twitched. "I heard. Hey, if you need anything…"

"Can you fix an espresso machine?" She turned on the heat full blast; arctic air shocked her face. She turned it off and huffed. It took entirely too long for vehicles to heat up. She should have moved farther south.

He ignored her rhetorical question, but the right side of his mouth inched north. In Aurora's book, that was a smile. Biggest one Beckett Marsh had ever laid on her. He adjusted the fleece collar of his sheriff's coat. "Still stands. It's my duty, you know. To protect people."

Yes, he reminded her every time she won a case. She was protecting people, too. People like her brother, Richie. Most of her clients were folks who needed a second chance to get it right. *Most*. She had to take the bad with good. Came with the territory.

Aurora hurried to the café and entered through the back. After fixing the espresso machine, she grabbed a caffè mocha and drove home for the night. She had work to do. Seven months ago Blair Sullivan, now McKnight, had asked her if she ever defended men like the ones who had come after Blair. The Mexican cartel. Aurora told her she didn't defend dead men. After those evil people had been taken down by the DEA, there weren't any left who needed a defense. It was an easy way to skirt around what Blair had really been asking, but the question had dogged her every day since.

When Richie committed suicide in prison, she didn't try to clear her older brother's name. He deserved as much, though. So, last month, she'd gone back to Richfield, Mississippi, where she'd been raised, opened up the old files and poked around. Nothing so far, but Richie was innocent and Aurora wasn't going to stop until she proved it. She owed him that much.

She parked in the drive and sprinted up to the porch of the antebellum home she'd rented from Mitch Rydell. The only things that belonged solely to her were the furniture inside and her car. She wasn't sure how long she'd get to stay in Hope, not with the possibility of Franco Renzetti coming after her. But it had been quiet this long and she'd put down a few roots.

She paused at the front door. Wind howled through stick-bare trees. Nights came sooner these days, and by four o'clock the sun had abandoned her. Beckett's warning and the gravelly-voiced threat sent her scanning her large yard and the tree line fifteen feet to the right. She shook off the jitters and went inside. Ah, delicious warmth and the smell of her cinnamon potpourri helped chase away the blues and the creeps. After drinking her coffee, then making a bite of dinner and poring over files and evidence, she stood and stretched.

The sound of a diesel engine roared in the near distance. Odd. Her road only had three other houses and hardly ever received traffic. She clutched her stomach, as if pressing her hand against it would send the fright and paranoia away, and tiptoed into the living room as the noise grew louder, closer.

She fisted her hands as blinding headlights shone on her house.

One more step forward, a high-pitched clang reverberated through her home and something crashed through her living room window.

Aurora shrieked, threw her hands up in defense and squeezed her eyes closed as the object careened into her shoulder and bounced off, landing on the floor and rolling across the hardwood.

The wind whipped relentlessly through the broken window, adding to the chill in her bones. Aurora stood stunned as she massaged the throbbing area.

Shards of glass covered her couch and a few specks skittered across the floor.

The blinding lights disappeared, leaving her yard draped in darkness.

She inched toward the object rolling on her hardwood floor. An empty bottle.

Old Crow whiskey.

Same brand Austin Bledsoe had been drinking when he sped through a stop sign and hit Bethany Russell.

Her hands trembled as she tucked them inside her sweatshirt sleeves, using them as gloves to pick up the bottle, a question rattling her brain and sending a thump of fear into her chest. She'd been threatened earlier. Was this the end or only the beginning?

* * *

"Counselor!" Beckett Marsh poked his nose through Aurora Daniels's broken windowpane when she wouldn't answer the front door. It had taken him ten minutes to get here after she'd called. While her words had come out clear, the speed at which she'd spoken told the tale.

She'd been shaken up.

Now she stood in the middle of her living room with one hand cupping her left shoulder. He did a double take. This wasn't the confident professional in her typical attire of power suits and heels. Bare feet anchored to the hardwood, baggy gray sweatpants and an equally baggy Ole Miss Rebels sweatshirt masking her slender figure. And still something about the look, even with her signature tight knot at the base of her neck, rattled something loose in his chest. He refocused, uncomfortable with the powerful response to seeing her like this. Not like he hadn't been attracted the first time he'd laid eyes on her a little over a year ago when he came back home. Anyone would be an idiot not to find her attractive. But her line of work put the kibosh on anything beyond admiring a beautiful woman. Ain't no way he could follow that trail. "You hurt?"

She hurried to the front door, unlocking it and letting him inside. "Just my shoulder. Probably going to bruise, is all." She gave it a haphazard rub. Nice attempt at the brave front.

That bottle could have hit her head, knocked her out, cut her up or worse. He fisted his hand to keep from touching her. "I got here as fast as I could."

"I appreciate it. Guess you were correct about the threats." She tossed out a weak laugh.

This was nothing to make light of, and he hated that he'd been right. He ignored the hint of chocolate and the faint scent of something flowery drifting from her skin or clothing. A bottle on the kitchen table snagged his attention. "Old Crow."

"Like I said when I called, they threw a whiskey bottle. Drove a big truck, big engine. Could be a Hemi V8. Maybe even a Detroit Diesel 550 horsepower. Heard it when it turned on my street."

Beckett inclined his head and studied her, unsure of what impressed him more. The fact Aurora Daniels had a handle on big engines or that she'd called him first—or at all. They butted heads often and he wouldn't deny he was pretty tough on her. But for every five people he tossed behind bars, she'd cut three loose with her slick litigation skills. How was he supposed to keep his county safe when the shrewd counselor put criminals right back out on the street?

He'd seen what monsters free to prey the streets could do. Seen evil get away with murder when one had claimed his fiancée's life the night before their wedding. Meghan's lifeless body had been seared into Beckett's mind forever. No matter how hard he tried, he couldn't forgive himself for not coming to her rescue in time.

"Sheriff?" Aurora drew him from the nightmare that plagued him. "I asked how many people on your end know that Austin Bledsoe was drinking Old Crow whiskey."

Good question. Same one that had popped into his mind. That brain of hers was incredible. Sharp. Too bad it wasn't being used for a better cause. "Officers on the scene the night Bethany Russell was killed. Whoever was working evidence. I can't think of anyone else. The judge."

Aurora quirked her lips to the side. "The Russell family and anyone they told."

Beckett's gut clenched. He couldn't rule out Trevor Russell or his teenage boy. But he hated to have to question them. They'd been through enough already with Bethany's death and funeral only four short months ago. They'd been clinging to the hope of justice today, but it had miscarried. However, he knew firsthand what time soaked in grief could do, and it wasn't pretty. He'd been on that end of the stick. "I'll talk to Trevor."

Aurora sighed and tapped her nail against the tip of her nose. He'd noticed that before. In the courtroom. Her thinking habit. "I guess I need to get some plastic over that. I can call Mitch in the morning. Have the glass replaced." She bounded for the door leading to the garage. Beckett followed.

"Plastic isn't safe. Anyone could cut through it."

Aurora paused. "I think that guy's threat at the courthouse today was meant to scare me. Mission accomplished. If he'd wanted to hurt me, he'd have already gotten into the house. If this was him."

Fire pulsed in his chest. "What threat?" Aurora had said she was used to unkind words, and he could easily imagine. She'd worked in a high-profile law firm that repped some shady clients. But a bottle had made direct impact on her body. This wasn't idle threats and unkind verbiage.

"A guy in the crowd today. I didn't recognize the voice and couldn't match a face to the words, but he told me to be careful or I could end up in a car accident like Bethany Russell. Just words." She shrugged, but Beckett wasn't born yesterday. Aurora was trying to talk herself out of being afraid. Fear wasn't always a bad thing. Fear had kept him alive and alert on all his tours and missions as a SEAL.

"Well, I'd feel better if we didn't use plastic. Besides, it's gonna get down in the twenties tonight. Plastic won't keep the nip out."

She pointed to the far side of the sparse garage. "I have some plywood. That work?"

"Yup. And you need to put some shoes on. Protect your feet while we get the glass cleaned up."

She pursed her lips but said nothing.

Beckett grabbed several boards in the corner and Aurora retrieved a hammer and nails and followed him inside. "Got a broom?"

"The one I use for sweeping or the one I ride on?" Aurora tilted her head and pierced him with a maybe sort of accusing glare.

So that's what she assumed he thought of her. Hardly. He wasn't sure what to think. This was the longest he'd spent in a room with her other than a courtroom, and they didn't converse much inside. Besides, he never allowed himself to see her as anything but the enemy. Now, she was a target who trusted him to protect her. And that's exactly what he planned to do.

"Sweeping will be fine." He smirked. "I don't want to put you out a vehicle."

"Hmm…" Aurora snagged a broom and dustpan from the pantry, slipped on a pair of house shoes that had been lying under the kitchen table, and they went to work cleaning up the glass and boarding up the window.

When it was finished he noticed her fire was dying. "You got any wood? I can get a fresh fire going before I head out." No way was he letting her do it. Instinct told him this wasn't over. But he didn't want to scare her further, and it didn't technically warrant putting a detail on her.

Meghan had begged and pleaded with the sheriff in her small Georgia town to patrol her house. But they couldn't prove she was in danger. Her stalker had been cunning, averting the law yet tormenting her. When it first started, Beckett had been on an extended tour in Afghanistan with Meghan's brother, Wilder. He'd had no idea, not until he came home. He'd been powerless.

He had the power to do something about this.

"I'll do a few drive-bys through the night. Make sure everything's safe." He might not be able to use taxpayers' dollars for a deputy to sit outside, but Beckett could on his own time.

Aurora met him with a delicate smile. "I appreciate that. But I don't think it's necessary, and I have some self-defense training, as well as gun-range time. I'm a pretty good shot."

Brave. Resilient. But Beckett had seen fear on thousands of faces. "I believe you, Counselor. Now, about that firewood?"

"Oh." She scratched at the base of her neck. A dainty neck. Smooth. "It's under the tarp on the side of the house, but I can do it. Really. I mean, I started that one."

"I don't feel comfortable letting you haul wood in out of the dark. Just in case. Precaution, is all." He flipped the collar on his coat up and stalked to the woodpile. Doing a slow scan with his flashlight, he checked out the woods that surrounded the house. No footprints. The branches rustled. Critters slunk around, crunching dead leaves. Something was off. Puffs of night air plumed in front of him as he patrolled the yard. He couldn't spot anyone, but red flags waved.

Someone was out there.

Watching.

Or maybe he was paranoid after what had happened to Meghan.

Beckett hauled in the firewood and a few extra logs. Inside, freshly brewed coffee uncoiled one of the many knots tightening his neck and shoulders.

Aurora handed him a steaming cup. "It's brutal out there. Warm you up. Least I can do."

He dusted his hands on his pants and accepted the cup, her fingers brushing his. He cleared his throat. "Thanks."

"It's black, like you like it."

He sipped, the French roast warming all the way down his throat. "You know how I like my coffee?"

"I'm in the coffee business." She shrugged, but her cheeks flushed a pretty shade of rose and she broke eye contact. First time for everything. She held his glares quite well in the courtroom or at the jail.

"Why are you in the coffee business? You seem

to be living in high cotton." Driving that BMW, wearing fancy clothes, and the air about her simply smelled like money. He took another sip and squatted by the fire.

Aurora folded her arms across her chest and gazed into the flames. "To be honest, the coffee in Hope stinks. I drink enough that it dictated opening up a business."

He snorted. "Uh-huh, now really, be honest."

"How do you know I'm not?"

Her upturned and perky nose might give off an appearance of snootiness, but the averting gaze and body language said she had a more private reason and didn't care to divulge. "I just know. But you don't have to get personal with me, Counselor." He stood and studied the few photos on her mantel. "That's you. Can't miss the hair." Blondish red. Probably still long like the toothless little girl in the photo; he'd never seen it down before. She'd grown from adorable to beautiful. "That a brother or something next to you?"

"Yes. Richie. He died."

The words punched his chest. "I'm sorry."

She clutched the photo and seemed to slip down memory lane. "He's why I do what I do. He committed suicide in prison when I was in my second year of law school."

Beckett grimaced. "Went to school to get him out somehow?"

"He was innocent. What choice did I have? Someone had to give him decent counsel. Who better to advocate for him than someone who believed in him?"

"Ninety-nine percent of criminals say they're innocent."

Aurora's eyes hardened and she set the photo back on the mantel. "Some are telling the truth. Like Richie."

Beckett had worn out his welcome, but that suited him. He wasn't diggin' seeing Aurora as a victim. A really soft, beautiful woman who grieved her brother even if he was a criminal. "Thanks for the coffee."

"When I clear his name, you'll be the first to know, Sheriff."

He opened the door and stepped onto the porch. "Lock it behind me and I'll be by a few times. If you need anything—"

"I can handle it myself." Brazenness and a need to prove her case held his gaze, but beyond that lay something else. Torment. Sorrow.

Okay, her view on the justice system got a rise out of him, but could he be a bigger idiot? He'd basically insulted her dead brother, whom she loved. What a jerk. He owed her an apology for his insensitivity.

"Look—"

Her cell rang. She held up an index finger and

snagged it from the table by the couch. She studied the screen and frowned.

Someone she didn't want to talk to? Beckett ought to go. He could apologize later. It was freezing out here. He should have moved to Florida. "I'm gonna—" The rest of his sentence nose-dived when Aurora's cheeks blanched. She hadn't said anything after her hello.

"Who is this?" Her voice trembled.

"What's going on?" Beckett whispered.

"Hello? Hello…" Aurora hit the end button and stared at Beckett, eyes wide.

Beckett reentered the house and shut the door behind him. "Who was that?"

"Same gritty voice from this morning. In the crowd." Her tone was too quiet, hollow.

Beckett's neck muscles wound even tighter and he ground his jaw. "What did he say?"

Aurora clutched her throat. "Death is coming for me."

TWO

Beckett snagged Aurora's phone and checked her recent calls. Unknown number. "I'll get a trace on this."

"We both know that's a long shot. Probably a burner phone." She rubbed her temples and pursed her lips.

She was right. But if someone had done this on impulse, they might have only blocked her view of the number. It was a thin thread, but he was hanging on to it. "No one is going to get to you, understand?"

Aurora's eyebrows tweaked and she gave a weak nod. She trusted him enough to call but not enough to actually protect her?

He pivoted her carefully, forcing her to face him. "*No* one." He drilled into her gaze until she gave a solid nod. Better. Beckett needed her to have faith in him. *He* needed to have some faith, but after his failure with Meghan, his faith in himself—and in God—was shaky at best. This time, he couldn't let someone take a life right out from under his nose. His trained nose. Guilt battered his ribs. "I'll call one of my guys to come and get the phone—"

"No." Aurora tapped her nose again. Something in that pretty head was cooking. "Someone on the inside knows what brand of whiskey Austin Bledsoe drank. I don't trust anyone in your office to do right by me. Sorry not sorry. You do it. I trust *you*, Beckett."

Beckett. He'd never heard her say his name. Not that he'd ever used hers. He liked the way it rolled off her tongue. "You sure?"

"I may not enjoy our conversations and you may not like me, but you're honest to a fault."

They didn't have conversations. They had arguments. And he'd never said he didn't like her. His fear at the moment was getting to know her and liking her too much. "All right. I'll do it myself." He didn't bother to acknowledge her other statement. "And I have to make a few stops."

"Question Trevor Russell?"

The woman was keen. "Yes." Not that he was over the moon about it. But the situation warranted it. Beckett couldn't take her with him. Couldn't leave her here unattended, and she didn't trust anyone but him, which made things difficult but also sent a swell of satisfaction through him.

"Can you have a friend come over? Or go somewhere for the night?"

Her mouth dropped open and defiance slashed through her eyes. "Let him win? Let him run me out of my own home over a scary phone call? Hardly."

He had a feeling she'd say something like that. She might as well be a walking billboard for the word *resolute.* He'd witnessed that time and again in the courtroom. Like a bulldog on a bone. "I can't protect you if I'm not here. He's already tossed a bottle through the window—and now the call. Maybe it *is* a threat to terrorize you." No way he believed that, based on personal experience. "But maybe it's not."

She ran her hands over her face and groaned. "Kelly's in Memphis for the night. New grandbaby."

Judge Kelly Marks had hired Aurora as the court-appointed attorney. From what Beckett knew, she'd been one of Aurora's law professors at Ole Miss and her mentor of sorts. She lived over by the Magnolia Inn, on the hill with an iron gate. Aurora would be more secure there, but that wasn't an option tonight. "What about staying with Holt and Blair McKnight?"

Aurora gave him a cutting eye. "They've been

married less than six months. I'm not intruding on the honeymooners."

Beckett growled. "It's one night. I'm calling them."

Aurora pinched the bridge of her nose. "I feel like a child. Like…like I'm losing."

"Not everything is about winning and losing, Counselor. This is about staying safe. Holt McKnight will make sure of it, and I trust him with my life. I trust him with yours."

Beckett gauged her. She was just shy of stomping her foot and crying or throat punching him. He eased back in case of the latter. Surely, she'd see reason and let him drive her over to the McKnights' for one evening. Tomorrow, she could stay with Judge Marks.

"Only for tonight."

His muscles relaxed in thankfulness they weren't going to butt heads again because, when it came to Aurora's safety, he'd fight until he won. He called Holt, gave him the lowdown and hung up. "Blair's making up the guest room now."

"Then one night, it is. I'm not going to run scared."

Beckett studied her. Seemed like that was what she'd done by coming to Hope. Why else would an uppity attorney like her move from Chicago to here? It was like she'd run as far away as she could from Franco Renzetti. "Nobody but you said you were. Pack a bag."

She muttered about his barking demands and trudged to her room.

Like a child. But cute as all get-out.

A few moments later, Aurora had a bag hanging on her arm. "I need to take that box of files. I can't risk someone knowing I'm gone and busting in here and ransacking the place—including the files."

Beckett collected the ones lying on the table and added them to the rest in the cardboard box. Case files on her brother. "Hey," he said, and turned, "I'm sorry for earlier. I know how much you loved your brother, and I basically told you he was guilty. I don't even know the facts. So, I apologize for acting like a jerk."

"Thank you."

Well, that was something he'd never expected out of the shrewd attorney. Grace. It surprised and befuddled him. Beckett carried the box to the door. "Ready?"

"Yeah."

"I'm gonna go out first. Do a sweep, make sure no one is lurking. I'll come back inside and get you." He grabbed her other bag and surveyed the area from the porch. After placing the items in the backseat, he swept the perimeter. Everything seemed quiet. Bleak. Temps were dropping steadily. A sense that someone was watching skittered across his flesh. *Please don't be you, Trevor.* He finished clearing the area and came inside. Aurora was perched on her recliner.

"Everything as it should be?"

He nodded. He'd leave the sixth sense to himself. "Let's go." He hovered over her as she locked the front door and sheltered her as they made their way to his Chevy Tahoe, the words *Fallon County Sheriff* reflecting in silver.

Ten minutes later, he had her on Holt and Blair McKnight's porch. Blair guided Aurora inside, and Holt stepped outside and closed the front door, his hair whipping in all directions as they stood in the frigid night. "What are you thinking?"

Beckett cupped his aching neck. "Could be anyone, man. She shook up a crowd today. People starting to heal. This motion brought everything back up."

Holt rested a hip on the wooden porch railing. "I'm sure Trevor was hoping for the court to rule in his favor. He's bound to be furious. Old wounds ripped open. But would he stoop to throwing a whiskey bottle through the window and threatening Aurora with that kind of phone call? He's a good dude. Lieutenant at the firehouse. Lot to lose if he did this."

"What if it had been Blair who Austin rammed into? What would you do?" Beckett tipped his head as Holt's face hardened. "Exactly. You'd want to see that kid pay for the rest of his life, and then some. And you'd want to see whoever let him walk pay along with him."

"He's not going to walk."

"He's not serving a life sentence, either. Probably get three months. Then community service and parole. Hardly seems fair." Beckett pulled a butterscotch candy from his coat pocket and popped it into his mouth, twisting the golden paper between his thumb and index finger. "I don't know. I'm heading over there now. Aurora doesn't want to be here. She says she's cutting into honeymoon time."

Holt chuckled. "Blair has morning sickness at night. The honeymoon is over, bro. They say she should feel better come next month. So, be glad Aurora was threatened now and not in April." He gave Beckett's shoulder a solid pat. "She'll be safe here. And she's welcome to stay till next week. But then I'm in Memphis for a few days teaching a narcotics class. I'd rather—"

"Her not be in the house with only Blair and your kiddo cookin' inside her. I wouldn't do that. She's staying with Judge Marks come tomorrow."

"I mean what's Blair gonna do anyway? Puke on the attacker?"

Beckett laughed. "I'll be by in the morning. Or if anything new arises." He shook Holt's hand

and left for Trevor Russell's house. Holt was right. With the ruling today, all that agony and hurt would be fresh. Trevor and his family had been banking all these months that Austin Bledsoe would be punished to the fullest extent of the law. As an adult. *God, why did You let him get away with this? Why didn't You move the judge to rule that he be tried as an adult? You can do anything You want. Turn the heart of a pharaoh. Soften a king. Why did You fail them?*

His phone rang as he pulled into the Russells' driveway. He glanced at the screen. Wilder Flynn. His oldest buddy from the SEALs. And Meghan's brother. No time to talk. Besides, Beckett didn't have an answer for Wilder. Moving to Atlanta to work with his elite team and seeing him every day would only remind him of Meghan. Of failing her. Beckett wasn't sure he could handle that. Too much guilt. Plus, he'd finally come home to a safer career, and his mother was on top of the Rockies. Going back into a high-risk occupation would knock her off the edge. Mama had no one but him to see to her.

He let it go to voice mail and climbed the steps to Trevor's porch. A light burned in the living room. He knocked. Waited. Knocked again.

Trevor's son, Quent, opened up. Definitely not sleepy eyed. "Hey, bud. Your dad in?"

"Why?" Quent's jaw hardened and he bristled. Why the need to go defensive?

"I need to talk to him."

"Quent, who's here?" Trevor came to the door, hair tousled, white T-shirt wrinkled. "Beck? What's going on?"

Beckett scuffed his toe along the wooden planks. "How you doing?"

"You're here at eleven o'clock at night to ask me how I'm doing?" He frowned. "How do you think I'm doing?"

Beckett massaged his achy neck muscle again. "I know it's not the verdict you wanted to hear—"

"Not even close," he hissed. "Why are you here?"

Beckett told him about the whiskey bottle and the phone call. "I was wondering if you might know anything about that? Tell anyone the brand, perhaps?"

Trevor gave a humorless laugh. "Really? Give me a break. My wife is dead. That punk is getting away with it and you want to question me about a bottle? I'm only sorry it didn't whop her upside the head and knock some decency into her. Quent, go to bed."

After tonight, Beckett wasn't so sure that Aurora wasn't decent. She was complicated. "Wait. I need to ask Quent if he might know anything." He inspected the boy. "Do you?"

"No," he barked. "And if I did, I wouldn't tell you. I hope she gets what's coming to her." He stomped off, and Trevor pinched the bridge of his nose.

The kid had a lot of anger. Could it have been him? Maybe, but not the threats. Aurora had said the voice was gravelly. *Trevor's* voice was gravelly. But lots of male voices had a rasp. "I'm sorry. I had to ask. It's my job."

"Yeah." Trevor closed the door in Beckett's face. Well, that went well.

Aurora hadn't slept much last night. Not that Blair's guest bed was uncomfortable, but she'd had too much on her mind. Today, she had an appointment in Richfield, Mississippi, with the detective who'd been assigned her brother's case and an interview with Gus's widow, Darla McGregor. She'd always believed that Richie hadn't murdered her husband, and Aurora had been grateful someone had been on her side. Maybe, after all this time, one of them might remember something they hadn't before.

Now she sat across from Beckett at The Black-Eyed Pea, picking at her eggs and toast. He'd shown up to the McKnights' home bright and early and told her he was on protection detail. He'd then dropped her at the office for an hour before picking her back up for breakfast. Apparently, this was where he ate his most important meal of the day. He didn't appear to be into cooking. Aurora fixed poached eggs every single morning.

Beckett gave her the facts on Trevor Russell's questioning last night while he peppered his grits. She hadn't expected Mr. Russell or his son to roll over and confess. And she wasn't sure either of them had been behind the incident, anyway. It could have been anyone. But she had mulled over a few things. "I've changed my mind."

Beckett perked up. "About what?"

"Staying with Kelly. I can't let a couple of threats keep me from my home, Beckett. It's silly. It's drastic."

"It's better safe than sorry." He pointed to her plate. "Eat your eggs."

Bossy much? She frowned. "Do you know why I choose eggs for breakfast, Sheriff?"

Confusion crinkled the edges of his eyes. "Protein?"

"No," she said, her voice clipped, as he scooped a forkful of grits. "I eat eggs every day to remind me that I'm not a chicken."

Beckett paused midbite, eyebrows rising toward his thick, dark hairline. Then he laughed. Loud. Rich. "And you eat them poached because there's some kind of symbolism to being in hot water?"

She ignored him because maybe on some weird, subconscious level there was.

But the laughter wasn't funny. No doubt Beckett Marsh feared no one and no thing. "When it got sticky—much stickier than this—in Chicago, you know what I did? I tucked my tail between my legs and ran here, taking Kelly's offer. She risked her neck to give me this opportunity. I'd made a mess of my career. And I only tell you this because you undoubtedly know it anyway."

"Fair assessment." He chuckled again.

"Nothing about this is funny." She was trying to explain why she couldn't up and leave her house over some small-town threat. This wasn't La Cosa Nostra, for crying out loud. It was an angry citizen. It would pass.

"You're right. Well…the eggs thing is a little funny. Do you really eat eggs every day? And for that reason?"

She simply glowered, making her point.

"Sorry." The amusement in his eyes said he wasn't.

"I'm not going to let whoever this is scare me. That's exactly what he wants." She held up her hand. "Before you say it, it's not about winning, but it kind of is. Not for the sake of winning, but to let this guy know he can't do this. He can't frighten me out of my home."

Beckett grimaced and put down his fork,

wiped his mouth. "I see your point. But threats shouldn't be ignored or taken casually. What if it wasn't a scare tactic? What if it's a warning of things to come?"

"We take precautions other than me leaving my house. Besides, if he can find me at home, he can find me at someone else's."

"True. But I don't want you far from me."

"Well, I'm going to Richfield today. To interview—" Her phone rang. Not again. Oliver Benard. Her old law partner from Chicago had been calling the last several days, and Aurora had been ignoring every single one, including the vague voice mails informing her they needed to talk. About what? The fact it was Aurora's fault his son had died at Renzetti's hands in that car explosion? Instead of taking Aurora's life, they'd taken Hayden's. Aurora had been so ashamed and guilty, she hadn't even attended Hayden's funeral.

Here she was talking bravery and she couldn't even take Oliver's phone call.

"What is it? Is that an unknown caller? Again?"

"No." Aurora pocketed her phone and sipped her juice. "Just someone I can't talk to."

Beckett buttered his toast. "Why?"

"I don't want to. Now, back to my day. I appreciate you picking me up from Blair's this morning. But I can't become your new sidekick. I have a life. I have work. And I have Richie's case to dig into, which is why I'm going to Richfield this morning."

"I don't like it. That's two hours away." He pushed his plate aside. "Put it off until tomorrow. I'll go with you."

Aurora sized him up. Most of the time she could read people fairly well. This was a man bent on doing what he said he would—keeping her safe at all costs—which meant he wasn't going to budge on this. "I'll make a few calls and see if we can reschedule. If not, I'm doing it today, Beckett. I've put off defending my brother long enough."

He pointed to her plate. "Choke down your courage and I'll get the check, then drop you at the courthouse."

Aurora groaned. "Are you going to escort me across the street to my office afterward, as well?"

A sly grin cruised across his face. "Not if you eat your eggs."

She huffed, but a giggle surfaced in her throat. She switched the subject back to his hovering over her like she was some sheep in need of a shepherd. "This might be extreme."

"You have no idea what extreme is, Counselor." Beckett motioned for Jace Black, co-owner of the establishment, to bring the check.

She did know extreme, but the way Beckett said it, Aurora had a sneaky feeling he'd seen things that had nothing to do with SEAL missions or war. Something he kept private. A need to know rose up in her. A wish he'd confide in her. Which was silly. The last two days were the most she'd ever personally spent with Beckett. But she was beginning to see a side of him other than surly and unsociable. A sense of humor for one. Considerate. Thoughtful. She admired those attributes. Too much.

He held the door open for her and led her to the Tahoe. At the courthouse, Aurora waved to Beckett as she entered, then she made her way to Kelly's chambers. She knocked and was met with an invitation to come inside. Kelly sat behind her mahogany desk, robed. Her short, silver chin-length bob framed compassionate eyes. "I'm about to head into court, but I'm glad to see you. I heard about the threats."

"From who?"

Kelly tented her fingers on the desk. "The town in general. Rumors were buzzing around the courthouse this morning."

"Oh. So, how is the baby?"

"A doll. I have pictures." Kelly beamed.

Babies. Once upon a time she'd wanted to get married and have children of her own. But Richie had gone to prison and she'd jumped onto a different path. No time for real relationships or children. She'd been focused on work and all her pro bono cases, which had been the biggest appeal of the position at Benard, Lowenstein & Meyer. "So, you heard about the calls or the whiskey bottle?"

Kelly's mouth dropped open. "I heard your car got keyed and someone knocked out a window at your place. What else is going on?"

Aurora shared the details.

Kelly sat quietly, then clasped Aurora's hand. "You should stay with me."

Aurora had no doubt Kelly would offer. "I'm fine. You know how this goes. It'll blow over." She hoped. "But I do need to vent about something. Oliver Benard has been calling me."

Kelly leaned back in her plush office chair. "So answer."

"I can't. I'm scared."

"Scared to answer a phone call, but brave enough to stay in a house alone with threats coming through your front window." Kelly pointed at her. "The invitation to stay with me stands. I think you're being foolish by not accepting. However, I understand why you want to stand your ground and thus proclaim you're not afraid of threats. But if they escalate…"

"I'll let you know and take you up on it. About Oliver?"

"Take his call. You never know. He might want to show you some grace."

Grace.

She didn't deserve it. His son was dead because

of her. "I'd rather crawl into a hole. What if he's not calling to offer me gracious words?"

"Why, after two years, would he call you if not to extend a little kindness?"

"Anniversary of his son's death is February fifteenth. Maybe he wants to make sure I remember." Like she could forget.

"Aurora." Kelly's motherly tone warmed her. Her own mother hadn't been too motherly, and she'd spent most of her time locked in her bedroom. At least, when she wasn't taking her antidepressants, which was most of the time. "Trust God to work on your behalf."

She'd trusted God once. Before Richie had been stamped *guilty*. Before Aurora had been. Before her world had crumbled all around her. It didn't seem like God was there for her at all. "I'm heading to my office. I'll think about what you said."

She was leaving Kelly's chambers as her phone rang.

Unknown Caller.

Did she ignore it?

Chills poked her spine, but she answered.

No one spoke, only breath filtering lightly through the line.

"I was doing my job. So back off. If you think I won't figure out who you are, then you're mistaken."

A dark and menacing laugh cut straight to her marrow. "We'll see."

The line went dead.

Had she seriously taunted this guy? Well, she wouldn't be confiding that to Beckett.

She crossed the street to her office on the corner, working to erase the creepy-crawlers scuttling up and down her arms and the back of her neck. She entered.

"Mags?"

Her receptionist wasn't at her desk, but the light was on and piano music played on the Pandora station. Maybe she had run to grab tea at the Read It and Steep shop.

She ambled down the hall to her office and unlocked the door. Aurora caught a whiff of something. A foreign yet familiar scent. Something possibly masculine.

Bizarre. A wintry whisper pricked her neck.

She eyed her office. The lid on the cardboard box housing files for Richie's case was loose. It'd been on tight before Beckett had driven her to breakfast. Heels clicking on the tile caught her attention, and she poked her head out the office door.

Mags came in, blond hair spiking all over her head. "Hey, boss. I'm trying this new blooming tea. Felicity talked me in…to… What's wrong?"

Aurora controlled the panic in her voice. "Did anyone come in while I was at The Black-Eyed Pea?"

"No. Why?"

"No reason." She ducked back inside her office and finished removing the lid on the file box.

They were out of order.

Someone had pilfered through them.

But why?

And who? And how had he gotten into her office when she'd locked the door before heading to breakfast?

Peeking out the window behind her desk, Aurora skimmed the street. Nothing. Was this something she ought to bring to Beckett's attention? If she did, he'd go right back on his spiel to stay somewhere else. Maybe she hadn't had the lid on tight, or the files organized.

No. She had.

And the scent lingering. That was new.

He needed to know—once she drummed up a defense in favor of not packing up and running scared.

She combed through the files. Nothing had been taken. She called the detective and Gus McGregor's widow and rescheduled, then met with a few clients.

At lunch, she wasn't as shaken up, and by the time Beckett picked her up for dinner, she had decided not to mention it. Yet. He seemed tense on the drive to her house. He pulled into her driveway.

"I really don't like this," he said.

Aurora plucked Richie's file box from the floorboard. "See you tomorrow morning. My appointment with Detective Holmstead is at ten."

"I know you heard me."

"What was that?" She slanted her head as if she couldn't hear.

He scowled. "I'm coming in to clear the house."

"Well, of course you are."

Beckett climbed out of the Tahoe and walked Aurora up to the front door. She unlocked it and he entered first. A few moments later, he deemed it safe and she kicked off her shoes. "See you in the morning."

He hemmed and hawed around, then left. She locked the door and lit the fireplace. By the time she had finished making a few notes to ask Detective Holmstead, it was nearly nine o'clock. A low whistle pushed through the small crevices in the plywood covering the broken window. The glass man was coming out the day after tomorrow.

She crawled in bed and watched the news until she couldn't stay awake. The phone rang, startling her from sleep. Glancing at the clock, she growled. Eleven o'clock.

Unknown Caller.

She ignored it, her nerves fraying.

It rang again.

Silence filled the house except for the hum of her heating unit kicking on. *Please leave me alone.*

The shrill of the phone came once more. She answered. "Stop calling. It won't change anything. And you're not scaring me." Lies. Lies. Lies.

Nothing but a low exhalation. She hung up.

He called back.

After a few more times, she turned her cell phone off and padded to the kitchen for some chamomile tea. She filled her teapot and set it on the stove to boil. Leaning against the kitchen counter, she focused on calming her pulse.

The kettle whistled.

The light above the stove flickered and died.

She peeked under the microwave. Bulb must have burned out. She switched on the kitchen light.

Nothing.

A sense of dread pooled in her gut. She crept into the living room and turned the switch on the lamp.

Darkness.

Might have tripped the circuit. She tiptoed down the hall, refraining from the instinct goading her to sprint. She entered her room and retrieved her gun and a book light. She wasn't the idiot heroine who walked outside without a weapon. She flicked the safety off and approached the garage to flip the breaker. Invisible fingers slid across her skin, raising goose bumps.

It's a tripped circuit. That's it.

Muted moonlight left a sliver across the frigid concrete floor. Aurora quivered. Maybe from winter monopolizing the garage. Maybe a fair amount of fear. Probably both. She hurried to the metal breaker box and shined the book light on the black switches.

Yep. Tripped circuit. She slid it left and back to the right, then relaxed. "Stupid breaker. You picked a fine time to fail me."

A whiff of that same scent from her office snaked into her nostrils.

Hairs stood on end, awareness hammering her like a gavel against the sound block.

No time to move or swivel toward the presence in the garage. A strong arm shrouded in a black jacket came around her torso, pinning her arms to her sides; a gloved hand sealed her mouth and nose.

Can't breathe!

Panic kicked in, sending a sour taste to her throat and leaving her light-headed. She still clung to her gun, but he had her across the forearms, pinned and unable to aim even at his foot.

Aurora stomped the attacker's toes as hard as she could, then bent forward, throwing him off balance. When he loosened his grip she swung around. A mask covered his face.

Bringing the gun up, she aimed, but he ducked

as she fired, then he tore through the door leading into her house.

The front door slammed.

Aurora bent at the knees and gulped for air.

The odd scent remained, and she couldn't quite place it other than that it had been in her office earlier.

Why would her attacker be interested in Richie's files? A frightening thought knocked her off balance.

What if the tossed whiskey bottle had nothing to do with the earlier calls and attacks? What if this had everything to do with her nosing into Gus McGregor's murder?

THREE

Gunfire!

Beckett knew that reverberating sound any-where. Instinct kicked in and he laid on the gas.

Three houses down from Aurora, a figure fled through the woods. Beckett threw the Tahoe into Park, leaped from it, drew his weapon and hauled his tail across Aurora's neighbors' yards in pursuit.

If the assailant was running, he probably wasn't injured, at least not fatally.

But Aurora might be.

He skidded to a halt and doubled back to Aurora's, his pulse pounding in his temples.

He cautiously opened her front door.

He should have fought harder—demanded she stay elsewhere, done a drive-by sooner, staked out her place. He continued to mentally kick himself as he inched through her house.

His phone rang.

He ignored it.

"Counselor?" he called from the dining room, then worked his way warily down the hall.

Training his gun on her bedroom door, he toed it open a crack.

A pop sounded and he hit the floor. "Aurora! It's Beckett!"

The door opened wider and she peered down at him, wild-eyed, gun in hand.

"Could you point that somewhere besides my head, please, ma'am?"

She slid her finger across the safety and lowered it. "Sorry. I tried to call you."

Must have been the call he ignored. He stood. She was safe. "I heard a gunshot and saw someone running from the house." He closed the distance between them and touched her cheek. "I'm sorry for letting you down."

She shook her head. "No. It's not your fault."

Except it 100 percent was. "What happened?"

Aurora bit her bottom lip. "You're going to be livid. I might have withheld some information."

"What information?"

"Before you start getting all alpha male on me, let me tell the whole story."

Alpha male? He'd laugh if he wasn't half scared out of his mind. "Fine."

She explained everything and with each word his blood pressure rose. "So you couldn't identify him?"

"Like I said, he wore a ski mask."

"And you're not holdin' back anything else? I know everything?" He clenched his teeth.

"Yes."

He restrained from blowing a gasket, balled and released his fists, then repeated. "So I don't need to remind you that if something else happens, even minor to you, I'm to be informed. *Immediately.*"

"Sir, yes, sir." She huffed.

She hated being bossed. He wasn't bossing. He was used to being in charge and people following orders. Aurora was a little alpha herself. Total type A. He'd have to work on his approach with her.

"Please," he offered as politely as possible.

She placated him. "I will."

Why would someone upset about the verdict yesterday dig through her dead brother's case files? What would be the point?

"Were your filing cabinets disturbed?" Maybe someone was hunting down a file on Austin Bledsoe.

"Not that I could tell. Not like Richie's files."

So it was probable that the other files hadn't been snooped through. He couldn't connect the dots. Frustration forced him to grind his jaw and growl under his breath. "Well, you can't stay here the rest of the night. I never liked that idea anyway. He could come back." Whoever *he* was.

"It's one a.m. I'd rather not wake up Kelly or the McKnights." She hung her head. "I can't believe I'm going to run scared."

"You're not. You're being smart and taking precautions. How did he get in your garage? Would you have heard it being manually opened?"

"Yes."

Beckett searched entry points while concocting a plan to protect her. At the bathroom, he stopped and pointed to the guest bathroom window. "Point of entry." Dusty footprints lined the tub. He gnawed the inside of his cheek. "I can have the bathroom printed."

"He wore gloves."

"Still." But she was right. It would probably be a dead end like she said would happen with the trace on her phone last night. Burner phone. Untraceable.

How long had this guy been inside her house, waiting until she went to sleep before creeping to the garage and tripping the breaker?

Aurora's wide eyes and pale cheeks testified that she was thinking the same thing. "I should have checked all my locks after the threats."

Beckett touched the windowsill. "See these slivers of wood and paint? He used something to pry it open. It was locked."

She gawked at the chipped sill.

"It's gonna be okay." He wasn't letting her out of his sight. Not for one second.

She nodded. "What do we do about the rest of the night?"

He'd been thinking about that. "I'd stay here, but I don't need any gossip. I'll take you to the Magnolia Inn. Pack a bag." He waited while she packed, then he loaded her up and drove her over to the Magnolia. Claire MacKay stood behind the desk sipping coffee.

"Hey, Sheriff. What brings you in this time of night?" She yawned and held up her cup. "I need a stronger brew."

"I need two adjoining rooms."

"Why?" Aurora marched up to the desk.

Beckett cut his eyes at her and she tilted her head, hesitantly resigning to the fact he was getting a room next door. Period.

"Fine," she grumbled.

"Anyone rings the desk or calls for Aurora, patch them through to my room." Beckett was taking every precaution.

"Of course." She handed them keys and didn't ask questions. He liked that about her. He was glad it wasn't her sister, Keeley, working tonight's shift. She was an entirely different story. "Breakfast is served from six until nine."

"You serve eggs?" he asked.

"We do." She gave him a puzzled expression.

"We'll be down for our courage at eight."

A puff of air escaped Aurora's nose and Claire stood befuddled. "Off with ya' then. Enjoy your sleep."

Upstairs. Safer. He led Aurora to her room and set down her bags, then unlocked the door leading to his room. "Don't lock this."

Her nostrils flared.

He'd ordered her again. "Please," he added.

Aurora sat on the edge of the queen-size bed. "I won't. Thank you, Beckett."

For what? Showing up late? "You defended yourself. Nice work, Counselor."

"I think you could call me Aurora. I'd be comfortable with that." She half smiled and his chest tightened.

"Aurora," he rasped. Felt entirely too right rolling off his tongue. "Doesn't fit." He tipped an invisible hat. "Night, Counselor."

She kicked off her shoes. "Night, Sheriff."

Beckett closed the door and laid his gun on the nightstand. What if Aurora hadn't been the shooter but the victim? The assailant had gotten into her house. Lain in wait. God had spared her life. Too bad He hadn't spared Meghan's. Didn't they all deserve to be rescued? Why did some receive help and some didn't? He'd been struggling with that question while trying to maintain his faith and trust in God. But the more he questioned, the more he doubted.

At 7:45 a.m. he knocked on Aurora's door. She opened it. The same dark circles drooped under her eyes as his and she was paler than usual, her hair pulled back in that tight knot on her neck. Her room held that flowery signature scent of hers. "Ready?"

"Yes. Thank you for accompanying me today. I know you have a county to take care of." She grabbed her purse and briefcase.

"Today, I'm taking care of you. No protests." He motioned for her to exit the room and he followed her downstairs where she ate poached eggs and he helped himself to a stack of pancakes. "We better hit the road if we want to make that ten o'clock appointment."

"I'd like to take my car. I don't want to make it obvious I'm investigating, and riding around in a sheriff's vehicle does exactly that—although by now all of Richfield knows. It's not much bigger than Hope." Aurora pulled her scarf tight around her neck as he paid, then they walked to the Tahoe.

"You want to drive your keyed car around? I can run it by Wallace's shop. Get it repainted. Set you up with a rental."

"I thought about having it fixed, but then I figured someone might do something else to it and I might as well wait until the threats die down and have it repaired in one fell swoop. Besides, I need whoever did it to know it doesn't bother me."

"You worry too much about what people think."

She clicked her seat belt in place and brushed invisible lint from her pant leg, then stared straight ahead.

Someone had done a number on her. Her false sense of security tugged at something deep within him. The pretty redhead wasn't fooling him. She was guarding herself from further pain. Pretending to be immune. A sudden urge to take that torment away knocked him full force. He shouldn't be having these feelings. Not for defense attorney Aurora Daniels. "We'll pick up your car and you can follow me to the station. I'll leave my vehicle there."

Twenty minutes later, they were on the road to Richfield, Mississippi. They made small talk, avoiding their professions. He talked a little about the navy. About his best friend, Wilder. She shared a few stories from law school and how she came to a vast knowledge about cars. Her grandfather and Richie had been mechanics. She'd liked spending time with them both. They hit 15 South and came into Richfield.

"So, I...didn't have a lot growing up. And I kind of got picked on in school. If you're expecting to see lots of hugs and me connecting with tons of friends, you won't. The day I graduated, I flew this coop so fast your head would spin."

Beckett couldn't imagine a woman as sharp, bright and beautiful as Aurora being bullied. "Financial status shouldn't dictate your social status. My mom and dad divorced when I was only three. He moved to California and pretty much wrote us off. I understand not coming from much. Mama worked three jobs and an extra part-time at Christmas to make sure I got what I wrote to Santa for."

Aurora's expression was knowing and kind. "If we got Christmas presents, we got them from my grandfather. But he died when I was fifteen. I admit, I'm kind of glad. Seeing Richie go to prison for a crime he didn't commit would have killed him."

He hadn't even asked. "What was he convicted of?"

Aurora heaved a breath. "Murder. Second degree."

Murder. Well, this brought the attacks into a new light. Aurora had mentioned that someone had been in her office nosing through her files. Beckett didn't like it, but he hadn't expected it to link to this case. If Richie was innocent—and Beckett wasn't so sure—then the real killer was out there. He was probably from this town and knew that Aurora was poking around.

"Can you give me the rundown of the case?" Beckett shifted in the passenger seat, his legs cramping.

"The file box is back there—grab it if you want. We're heading to a café to meet with Detective Holmstead."

Beckett grabbed a thick folder from the box and flipped it open. "Dwight Holmstead?"

"Yep."

Beckett skimmed the contents. "Gus McGregor. Killed in his own shop. Blunt force trauma to the back of the head. Murder weapon was a wrench."

"They didn't find any prints except Gus's and Richie's, but he employed four other mechanics. Any one of them could have worn gloves. Or they could have used another wrench and planted that one at the scene of the crime."

Beckett had some doubt. "Gus's blood was found on this wrench and it was lying near the body. That's clearly the murder weapon."

Aurora white-knuckled the wheel. "Not enough blood to determine if it was the murder weapon, but enough to prove he had indeed bled on it. Not even a trace of scalp or skull. There could be another weapon out there. With *more* than a few traces of Gus's blood. But the public defender didn't even bring that up. And why would someone leave a murder weapon lying right there?"

Beckett grunted as he scanned statements from

four witnesses stating Richie had been in the local bar drinking—inebriation would be a great reason to leave a murder weapon on the scene—and spouting off that Gus had swindled him out of several hundred dollars of pay. "A witness testified that she heard Richie say he was going over to Gus's to 'get his.'"

"So what. He didn't go, and no one can validate that he did."

"Can't prove he didn't."

She huffed as she whipped into a parking lot. "Can you not say anything? You're here as a…a bodyguard not a lawman. In fact, maybe come in ten minutes after me and sit at a table alone."

He laughed. "This is a small town. You think people aren't gonna figure out we're together because we sit at separate tables? I'll be quiet."

She snorted and snatched the file from Beckett. "I'm here to establish my brother didn't do it. Remember that."

"Noted." He pointed to his temple. "Like an elephant, I am."

"I'd go with mule, but…" She smirked and stepped into icebox-like weather. Beckett followed her inside the small café. The smell of spices, down-home cooking and camaraderie clung to the air. A few patrons acknowledged them, then returned to their meals and conversation.

An older man—average height, thick gray

hair and curious eyes—waved at Aurora. Beckett trailed behind and waited for her to make introductions. She introduced him to Dwight as her colleague, Beckett Marsh. Beckett held in a laugh. Dwight sized him up and nodded, then offered them a seat and encouraged them to order a piece of pie. Chocolate. Beckett accepted.

"Aurora, I appreciate your tenacity, hon. I do. I'm sorry for what happened to Richie, but this case is cut-and-dried."

Hon wasn't going to fly with the counselor. She'd see it as patronizing.

Aurora bristled.

Yep.

She stretched across the table, palms down. "Dwight, I don't care if you appreciate me or not. Richie didn't kill Gus. I know he got in a fair amount of trouble. I know you often hauled him home instead of tossing him in the clink. But that doesn't mean he was a murderer."

Dwight mashed a few piecrust crumbs onto his fork and slid them into his mouth. "I don't know anything new."

"Gus gambled. I know it all happened in the back of his garage, and several citizens of Richfield, who would be sorely ashamed if the news got out, joined in. One happens to be a deacon of a local church. Don't deny it. My one source is reliable."

Who was her source?

"Yet, he wasn't questioned," Aurora continued. "None of those men were. What if Gus cheated them out of money like he did my brother?"

Dwight handed his plate to the server as she set Beckett's pie in front of him. When she left, Dwight clucked his tongue in his cheek. "They played some cards. So what? It was all friendly. The evidence points to Richie. He had motive."

"He wasn't there that night! His prints were, and they should have been. He was employed at Gus's Garage."

Aurora had a valid point. Every avenue should have been run down. "How serious were these games? How big of a pot?" Beckett asked.

Aurora shot him the evil eye. "Elephant, remember?"

"Clearly, I don't." And he was on her side. At least, in this line of questioning. He turned to Dwight. "Why weren't those men questioned?"

"We didn't need to. I doubt the pot was that big."

"Well, how do you know if you didn't attend?" Aurora asked. "Or did you participate, Detective? Are you letting those men off to hide the fact you gambled?" Aurora opened her hand and began tapping each finger. "Illegal gambling. Detective. Deacons. Town officials."

Beckett cringed. With every word, Aurora

painted a target on her back. The flush on Dwight's neck reached to his hairline. "You're crossing the line, missy. I'm here out of sympathy, but you're killing it."

"I'm simply trying to understand why you wouldn't do your job." Aurora's nostrils flared.

"I'm done here."

Aurora opened her mouth, but Beckett laid a hand on hers. They watched as Dwight Holmstead stormed from the café.

"Tell me that's not shady, Sheriff."

Beckett pushed his pie away and rubbed the stubble on his chin. "I'll admit it. That's shady, Counselor."

"And notice he didn't admit or deny being a part of the poker games."

"I noticed." Richie may have killed Gus Mc-Gregor. But the detective was definitely hiding something, even if it was simply incompetence on the case. Would that give him motive to scare Aurora, to attack her?

The detective had a raspy voice.

Beckett wasn't ruling out anyone.

Aurora stood on Darla McGregor's doorstep, the garage where Gus had been murdered across the street. Beckett stood beside her. Maybe he was starting to believe her. He had admitted to Dwight's shadiness. If she could come up with other regulars at those poker games, it would be a big help. But Richie had been her source and he was gone. Small towns had a way of locking their secrets in vaults and tossing away the keys.

Darla opened the door and invited them into her worn-out but tidy home. Aurora introduced Beckett as a colleague again, and for the second time he flinched. The last thing he wanted was to be portrayed as someone who defended those accused of crimes. They sat on Darla's threadbare couch and Beckett kept silent as Aurora fired questions. No, Darla hadn't been in town that night.

She hadn't known about Gus's poker games. He'd kept most of his life private.

Beckett's eyes narrowed a fraction at that answer. Not buying it? Aurora wasn't so sure. Gus could have concealed the games easily and, if he'd won, said the money came from work. But if he had held them in his garage, wouldn't Darla have seen all the cars? Why lie?

Aurora pressed her hands together in a prayer-like gesture against her chest. "Can we browse the garage?"

Darla grabbed a set of keys lying on the nicked coffee table. "I had a feeling you'd want these. I don't know what you think you'll find after all these years."

Aurora wasn't sure, either. It had been over a decade since Richie went to prison. But she needed to do it. Should have done it a long time ago. "Probably nothing."

"Little Gus tinkers out there. Does some side work. But he's not here today. Those are his keys. I never go in that place anymore."

"Tell Little Gus thanks for us then," Aurora said. At thirty-two, Little Gus didn't need to be called that anymore, but names stuck. "We won't disturb anything, and thank you. For talking and for always believing in Richie's innocence. If you think of anything else, please call me."

Darla ran her hand through her hair, streaks of gray more prominent than the brunette, and handed Aurora the keys to the garage. "I'll tell him."

Beckett followed her across the street to the old mechanic shop. Dirty, run-down. Smelled like motor oil and years of neglect. "I wondered why the widow of the deceased would talk to you."

"She never thought it was Richie, but it didn't matter."

Emotion lodged in her throat as they stood inside the garage. A man had died here. She'd been so focused on Richie and his innocence that she hadn't allowed herself to think much about Gus. No one deserved what had been done to him.

"What do you hope to find?" Beckett asked.

"Something to grasp on to. We need to find out

who played in those games. Even if we get town gossip, some of it will be true. Always is."

"Can you ask your parents?"

"I don't talk to them much." Another reason to feel guilt and shame.

"Why?"

"Why do you want to know?" This conversation, if continued, wouldn't be considered small talk. And Beckett was only here to fulfill his duty. No point in getting to know her personally. When this was over he'd go back to scowling and blaming her for allowing justice to misfire. Sadly, oddly, she wished things were different. She shoved the feelings aside.

"I guess I'm… I don't know." He shrugged and stared at the wall, then focused on her. "I haven't talked to my dad since he left. He never called. Started a new life. Had a new family. He never responded the few times I did contact him. Not even when I went into the navy."

Aurora gawked at his blurted admission. Her dad hadn't walked out, but that didn't mean he'd been present in her life. She sympathized with Beckett, and he'd made an effort to reach out. Why? Didn't matter. He had and she wanted to reciprocate.

She hated to admit the truth about her less-than-ideal childhood, but fair was fair. "We lived in a trailer on the other end of town. Sometimes my dad worked. Sometimes he didn't. Mostly he drank. My mom is bipolar. When she's on meds she does well. But part of the time she thought she didn't need them and the other part she said she couldn't afford them, so she didn't take them often." She toed the dirty concrete floor. "Richie struggled with depression, too. Being convicted of Gus's murder and enduring the hardships of prison sent him spiraling into a dark place. He'd written me a few desperate letters. I kept telling him to hang on. I was working hard. I was going to save him."

She held back tears and shook her head. "I couldn't do it in time. I contacted the medical personnel at the prison, begged them to put him in solitary to protect him but…I failed. You know how that feels?"

Beckett eased into her personal space, a new expression in his eyes. Compassion. "Yes," he whispered. "I know."

What had Beckett Marsh ever failed at? He seemed to have it all together. He was tough. Intelligent. Strong. But the way he said he knew what failure felt like… Something in his past had shattered him. The raw honesty in his voice connected with her in a profound way. "Beckett, I'm so sorry—"

A creak overhead sounded and the connection was lost. "Did you hear that?"

Beckett slid his gaze upward and scanned the loft area. "Probably just the old building settling in the cold."

He was probably right. "I'm jumpy."

"With good reason." Beckett rubbed his hands together. "It's freezing in here."

"Tell me about it. And it gives me the creeps. I used to be at home in places like this, but now all I think about is how a mechanic shop ruined Richie's life."

Beckett shoved his hands in his pockets. "You were just a girl. You couldn't get through school any faster than you did."

"I know, but—"

A rattling echoed through the shop. She snapped up her head in time to see an engine attached to a chain plummeting toward her.

"Aurora!" Beckett hollered.

A rush of air smacked her face.

She couldn't move.

Beckett dove on her and rolled her across the frosty concrete as the engine crashed with a deafening clang. Dirt and grime exploded into a cloud surrounding them.

Pieces of metal busted loose and flew across the shop; Beckett covered Aurora's head with his strong arms, shielding her from debris and motor parts. A metallic and dirty taste coated her tongue and gagged her. She pinched her mouth closed.

Her entire body shook, but he continued to guard her, his arms like a mighty fortress, and nothing in this entire world could get past them to hurt her. With her belly to the floor, she coughed and shifted, peering up at Beckett. Amber eyes stared into her face, pupils dilated, his breath puffing against her nose and lips.

"You saved me."

"Barely," he rasped, and brushed a thumb across her cheek. He held it up. Grime had streaked her cheeks. "Did I hurt you?"

"No." Her head swam. Fear. Adrenaline. And something she didn't want to acknowledge.

He held her gaze a beat longer than what might be appropriate, then lifted his weight from her. "Stay here." He drew his weapon and bounded up the stairs, disappearing.

Aurora sat up, drew her knees to her chest and hugged them. On the floor lay a shattered engine and a pile of chain that had once held it in place. Could it have been faulty? A coincidence? An accident? She couldn't control her quaking, not even when she bit down on her bottom lip and gripped her knees tighter.

"The back door up here is open. The stairs and surrounding area are clear, but those creaks weren't the building settling and popping. Someone was here. Watching. Listening." He pointed to the tall row of tool chests. "Maybe taking cover from behind there."

Aftershock rippled through her muscles.

He grabbed a portion of the chain on the concrete. "It's been cut. And it's greasier than it should be."

"But it was directly above us. How did we not see someone standing up there cutting through a metal chain? Let's say someone did lube it to cut down on noise—we'd still have seen him."

"True." Beckett skimmed the area with narrowed eyes, then picked up a hacksaw from a tool chest. "But if he knew we'd be coming in here, he could have cut through it halfway while we were across the street."

"But there's no guarantee I'd be standing under it. That it would even fall while we were here."

Beckett's expression darkened. "Except he stuck around long enough to make sure. It'd only take one finger to give it a little push. That was most likely the creak we heard." He tromped down the metal stairs. "We were either followed, someone knew we'd come here, or your girl Darla might not think Richie is so innocent, after all."

"It wasn't Darla. She would never make a calculated move like that." Although she would have known she could cut halfway through the chain before they got there, and she did have a good idea they'd come into the garage, which is why she'd secured the keys for them. She could have come up the back stairs and given it the final push. But that was a major stretch.

"Don't be so quick to declare her innocent, Counselor. I know it's your job—"

"Don't go there." She met his menacing challenge. "Innocent until proven guilty."

"Well, let's go talk to her, shall we? Maybe she called someone and *innocently* mentioned you were here."

She bit her tongue, not liking his condescending and skeptical tone. Had his tours in the war hardened him, or was he always this quick to judge?

They crossed the street in silence. Darla answered the door and Beckett stole the lead, asking if she'd called anyone or told anyone about the interview scheduled today.

"No one but Little Gus and Linda." She motioned them inside. "Let's get you cleaned up, Aurora. I'm so sorry. Are you sure it wasn't an accident?"

"No," Beckett firmly said, "it wasn't."

"Who else has a key to the place?" Aurora asked and declined a rag. She was ready to go, to keep Beckett from breathing fire down Darla's neck.

"As far as I know, just Little Gus, but that door upstairs could have been unlocked." Darla gnawed on her nail. "He wouldn't have done this, Aurora. You know that, and I don't know anyone who would."

Aurora believed her. She couldn't let the clients who'd failed her with their guilt cause her to have a cynical outlook. She had to believe the best in people. She needed to.

"Who's Linda?" Beckett asked.

"My sister."

"Where does *she* live?"

"Beckett!" Aurora snapped. Because two women in their fifties were going to sneak around cutting metal chains and dropping engines on attorneys and law enforcement. *Give me a break.* She'd win that case standing on her head.

Beckett stood toe-to-toe with her glare. Then his jaw relaxed, and he seemed to acquiesce to her non-verbal argument of how ludicrous that would be.

He turned back to Darla. "And you haven't seen anyone lurking out there?" He loomed over her, not relenting on his intimidation techniques.

"No. I promise." Darla stumbled back a step as if she might faint.

"If you hear of anything—any talk about Aurora being here in the garage—call us. No one should know that information but you and the two people you shared it with. And, hopefully, they won't talk." Beckett gave her a stern eye.

"I won't say a word. Aurora, you sure you're not hurt?"

"I'm fine. Thank you." She could kick Beckett for terrifying Darla. She wouldn't hurt a fly.

Aurora followed Beckett outside. Her hands shook as she unlocked the car. Beckett wrapped his hands over hers, stilling her. "Why don't you let me drive? Give you a chance to calm down."

She paused, irritated, but considered the offer. And it had been an offer, not a command. "Good idea." She hustled to the passenger side and slid in. Her nerves were shot. What she thought would blow over had turned into a tornado of violence. Who could have done this?

"Do you think it was Gus's killer?" Aurora asked. Did Beckett believe her now?

"Or someone followed us. Not that you'd have to have knowledge of cars to cut through a chain, but it could be someone who has knowledge." Beckett rubbed his lips together. "I don't want to say it, but—"

"Trevor Russell's father owns a mechanic shop in Hope." Aurora covered her mouth with her hand.

"We can't be sure who is after you yet. But it's evident that someone is. And they don't want to scare you."

No, they wanted to shut her up.

Permanently.

FOUR

Beckett hadn't meant to incite another level of fear in Aurora, but the way she'd kept her hands balled in her lap and her mouth quiet for the last hour told him that's exactly what he'd done.

He'd taken the time of silence to work scenarios out in his head. The only one that made sense was that Aurora might be onto something about Richie's innocence. The evidence pointed to Richie, though. However, there must be something out there someone knew could be found, or they wouldn't have threatened or attacked Aurora. The question was what? And how were they going to figure it out?

Still, Beckett couldn't rule out Trevor or his son. He doubted another citizen would go to the extreme of following them to Richfield and cutting the chain on an engine hoist, but it wasn't out of the realm of possibility for Trevor or Quent. Beckett knew the lengths a person would go to seek vengeance. Justice.

Too far.

Aurora's phone rang and she flinched.

"You want me to answer it?" he asked.

"No," she rasped. "I know who it is this time." She silenced the ringer and tucked the phone in her pocket.

"In my experience, avoiding phone calls means someone wants to talk about something you don't." He ought to know. "Is it anything that might shed new light to the situation we're in, or the case?"

She rubbed her slender hand across her thigh. "I feel bad it's a 'we' situation. You could have gotten yourself killed knocking me away from that engine. You know that, right?"

Was that why she'd been so quiet? Not fear but guilt? Or both? "It's—"

"Your duty. I know. Doesn't make me feel less guilty. But I do thank you."

Ah. Guilt. And a fair amount of fear. *Was* it just his duty? Something about that engine falling had sent his heart into a dizzying spiral. When was the last time he'd been that terrified for someone? That worried? That desperate to protect?

His chest tightened and he clutched the wheel. Meghan.

"So you want to talk about who was on that phone?"

His phone rang. Beckett peeked at it lying on

the console. Wilder Flynn. "Can you hit the decline button for me?"

Aurora paused and gawked at him but then hit the red button. "Who are you avoiding?"

Beckett sighed. "A friend who keeps offering me a spot on his team. Shoving it at me, really."

Aurora perked up and shifted in her seat. "What kind of team? Where?"

He hadn't talked about it with anyone. Briefly, he'd tossed it out to Mama while having Sunday dinner, but she'd ignored him as if it wasn't worth hearing. Which meant it bothered her—him going off again to potentially hazardous assignments. He owed her a few years of peace.

But he'd been pressing Aurora to open up, and fair was fair. He brushed off the fact he had a strange desire to confide in her. "Well, since you're a lawyer, you have to keep it confidential, right?"

"Only if you put me on retainer." She rubbed her thumb against her index and middle fingers.

"Saving your life counts as currency, I'd think," he teased.

"I suppose it does. Did you ever imagine having me as your attorney?" Her mouth opened as mock surprise filled her face.

He chuckled. "Certainly not. But I don't need a defense to decline this offer. I have one. I just need Wilder to take the hint."

"Wilder?"

"Flynn. My best friend. We were SEALs together." His voice strained as he fought to control his emotions. "And I was engaged to his sister Meghan."

"Oh." Aurora tapped the end of her nose. "Didn't work out between you? Afraid you'll have to see her if you move down there?"

Grief washed over him like white waters. "No," he murmured. "She died the night before we got married."

Aurora rubbed his bicep. The small gesture eased the soreness. "I'm so sorry, Beckett."

He gave a solid nod. What was there to say? *It's okay?* It wasn't okay. Beckett could have saved Meghan, but he'd gotten there too late. He'd ignored his instincts earlier in the night to force her to stay in the same room with him for protection. Who cared about gossip? Who cared what people thought when she could be in danger? Who cared about traditions? But she'd thrown up every one of those. They were entering a pure marriage, and she didn't want anyone to think they weren't. Plus, yada, yada, yada, and he'd caved, knowing she'd been sent flowers that morning at the bed-and-breakfast with a note, reminding Meghan she belonged to someone else and demanding that she break off the wedding.

He had thought being across the yard in a small guest cottage would be enough.

But it hadn't been.

"Beckett, I didn't mean to force you into talking about what is clearly a painful memory. I apologize."

For a shrewd, tough attorney, Aurora was turning out to be a very tender woman. He almost wished she wouldn't be. It'd make the conflicting feelings inside him easier to deal with.

"Meghan had been stalked for a year. The first several months, I was on a tour and didn't know. But during the last two, I was home. I popped the question at the airport. Impulsive, but I knew what I wanted."

"To spend the rest of your life with her."

He clenched his teeth and gained some composure. "We went to dinner later that night. Afterward, I paid the bill and Meghan headed to the front door. A man approached her, and I could tell she was uncomfortable. I wasn't sure if it was the intimate way he got in her face and touched her or if it was because of me seeing it."

"She was cheating?"

"No. She was being stalked. But I caused a scene with the guy." He regretted that. Beckett was sure it was what had triggered the stalker's swift aggression and violence. "She told me it had been going on awhile. Didn't want to worry me.

So the couple of times I'd called her while overseas, she'd never mentioned it."

"What did you do?"

"I found him and had more words." Mistake. "He was the mayor's son. So guess what?"

"No one did anything about it." Her sour tone rang clear. She understood. According to her, no one had done anything to help Richie, either. After the interview earlier with Detective Holmstead, Beckett believed her.

"No, they did not. But I got a warning. And a lecture on PTSD." Anger surged again. Not that he didn't have some PTSD, but that hadn't been fueling his rage against Parker Hill, the stalker turned murderer. "Then in the middle of the night, he got into her room and strangled her. I was less than fifty feet away."

"I don't know what to say," she whispered, then exhaled. "So this offer?"

Relieved she'd moved on from that tragic night, Beckett sighed. "Wilder started a crisis-management firm after she died. In Atlanta. He was gonna go into private security anyway, but it's how he's dealt with her death. He's got a great team and a great reputation. They're doing excellent, but…"

"You'll be reminded every day of losing her. And not being able to help her."

Aurora had nailed it on the head. But, also, the tasks at times were high risk, and he had Mama to think about. And after what he'd almost done to Parker Hill…could he even trust himself if he got emotionally involved in a case?

"Something like that," he said.

"It's not your fault, you know."

He exited the ramp. "It's not yours, either—about Richie dying in prison." Seemed they had exceedingly more in common than he'd imagined. Pain. Loss. Regrets. Outrage.

"Maybe not—"

A terrible noise screeched through the car and the steering wheel shuddered.

"What's happening?" Aurora hollered and braced herself.

The car jolted and Beckett put some muscle into the steering wheel.

"Beckett!"

They were headed straight for the overpass.

He focused and fought to control the car and keep it from going over the side. If he could get to the edge.

Metal scraping against concrete sent sparks flying around the driver's side.

They'd lost a wheel.

"Hold on, Counselor!" he managed as the passenger side of the car smashed into the concrete guardrail, metal now crunching. Aurora shrieked.

He guided the car past the overpass and careened into the ditch, narrowly missing a tree. He braked and they lurched forward, Aurora letting out a hiss as the seat belt cut into the tender skin around her neck.

Beckett freed her from the constricting belt and tilted her head to the side for a better inspection of her injury. Blood had already surfaced, and skin had been rubbed away. He touched the wound and she winced. "Sorry."

"I'm fine." She groaned and rubbed her thigh.

He pointed to her leg. "Are you hurt? Do you need me to take a look?"

"No." She sucked in her bottom lip. "It'll be okay."

"I wish I could have guided us better." Wished he could have kept her from being hurt altogether.

"Beckett, what you did was incredible."

He opened the driver's-side door, hopped out and then leaned in, reaching for her. "Your door isn't going to open. Come on."

She maneuvered herself in his direction. He placed his hands under her arms and lifted her out of the car. "You sure you're all right?"

"I'm a little the worse for wear, but alive. And thankful." Her arms rested on his biceps. He didn't make a move to back up. She didn't, either. After a few beats, she broke contact. "Did we have a blowout?"

Beckett squatted and examined the front driver's side where the wheel was missing. He viewed the wheel studs and ground his teeth. "No. Someone loosened the lug nuts."

"What?" She bent at the knees, inspecting. "You're right. The wheel studs aren't broken off. If it'd been a blowout, they would have been." She shivered. "If I'd have been driving…I don't know if I could have controlled the vehicle like you did. I would have gone straight off the overpass. I would have—"

He cut off her sentence by wrapping his arms around her, offering her comfort. "Don't go there. You're here. You're alive. And we're going to get who did this."

She burrowed into his chest and he smoothed her hair until she finally spoke. "They had to have done this a day or so ago. It'd take that long for the lug nuts to release."

This woman knew her cars. He couldn't control the flare of admiration and attraction. "You're right."

"That night you chased the attacker. What if he'd loosened my lug nuts before entering my house?" She broke away from his embrace and wrapped her arms around her middle.

The time line matched.

"It's likely. We'll print your car, but…"

"Probably find zip. I know. Just like no prints on my bathroom window. No hits on the shoe treads you took from my bathtub or the trace on my phone."

"Well, you were right about one other thing, too," Beckett said as he drew his phone to call a deputy to pick them up. They were about twenty minutes from Hope.

"What's that?"

"The jerk wasn't finished with your car. Be thankful you didn't fork out the dough to have the paint fixed."

She stared at him a moment and chuckled before it turned into a full-blown belly laugh. He laughed with her until the dispatcher answered.

Sighing, she leaned back against the car and quivered. He hung up and shrugged off his coat, wrapping it around her.

"You'll get cold," she protested.

He ignored her and tugged it tighter. "We could get in the backseat. Warm up."

"I beg your pardon." Indignation rose in her voice.

Beckett held up his hands. "I mean inside, where Old Man Winter can't beat us to death."

The offensive glare transformed into graciousness. "After you."

"No, after you." He opened the door and she crawled inside the car. No, he wasn't going to put his arms around her and bring her warmth, but the yearning to do so needled his ribs, along with the worry that the attacks were escalating by the second and he had to do whatever was necessary to protect Aurora.

Aurora sat at the small corner table of Sufficient Grounds nursing a caffè mocha. She'd finally thawed out after the twenty-minute wait for Deputy Ferrell to arrive. Beckett had vouched for him, but Aurora had a hard time trusting anyone. She rolled her head around, working the stiffness from her neck. Her thigh was tender, but other than that she was operating on all cylinders.

Beckett had her car towed, but it was totaled. Guess he was now her new chauffeur. Not that she couldn't rent a car, but what was the point when he'd pretty much declared he was her new bodyguard? Surprisingly, she didn't mind. Not that she wasn't a strong, capable woman. But it was nice to have a man like Beckett come to her aid and show some chivalry. She closed her eyes. Could still smell the scent from his warm coat. Sweet and woodsy.

"What are you all off in la-la land about?" Blair McKnight stood with a hand on her nonexistent baby bump.

"Nothing. Have a seat. You here for a coffee?"

"Fake coffee."

"Decaf?"

"Ugh. Just put my order in." She sat across from

her. "I know that look, Aurora. I've had that look. I still get that look."

Heat filled Aurora's cheeks. "And what look is that?"

"You're smitten."

Aurora snorted. "I don't get smitten."

Blair slanted her eyes and poked a finger at her. "You do now. Because you are. Beckett's a great guy. He can be intense sometimes, but that's because he takes his job seriously."

There might not be a truer statement.

"He's not seeing anyone, either. Maybe he hasn't met the right woman." Her tone was laced with all sorts of innuendo.

No. He had. She'd been killed or he'd be married right now. Speaking of right now, Aurora wasn't comfortable with this conversation. She wasn't smitten. She was too levelheaded. She was attracted to Beckett, admired and respected him. Appreciated him. But she wasn't smitten. She couldn't be.

At the end of the day, they worked on two different sides of the law. They didn't see eye to eye, and that would never work. Who knew, he might decide to move to Atlanta when all was said and done, which left her with an unsettling feeling. Hope wouldn't be the same without Beckett Marsh.

"I didn't mean to upset you, Aurora. I was teasing. Well, not really. You do seem smitten. Or… you did. Now you have *upset* written all over your face."

"No. I mean, I am upset." She told her what had happened earlier. "But I can't stop investigating. I have to bring justice to Richie's name. I owe him that. He deserves it."

Blair gripped Aurora's hand. "I understand. I'll be praying for you and Beckett. You know, you may not know who is doing this, but God does. So I'm believing He'll lead you guys to the savage and keep you safe in the meantime. I'm so sorry this is happening to you."

Blair had been through a lot when the cartel had come after her. It's when she'd fallen in love with Holt. "Thank you for the prayers." She wasn't sure they'd reach heaven's ears. She'd prayed God would help Richie hold on until she could come to his aid. But He hadn't heard. Or had chosen not to listen. He'd let Richie die, an innocent man deemed guilty.

She needed a subject change or she might break down right here. And Aurora Daniels didn't have breakdowns. Although she'd come close after the car wreck, when Beckett's arms had lifted her into his safety and comfort. "How did you know you were in love with Holt and not just appreciative of him or swept up because of all the drama? I mean, it's hard not to admire a man who's sacrificing his life for you." Not that she was in love with Beckett. Hardly.

Blair laid her hand on her chest. "A man who's willing to sacrifice his life for you is more than worth admiring. He's worth loving. If it's going down that road, you'll know."

Katelynn called Blair's name and she stood.

"Hey, you won't—"

"Say anything to Holt? No way. Us girls got to stick together. Besides, he'd just shrug and say, 'Sweet. What's for dinner?'" She laughed and strolled to the counter.

If she and Beckett didn't have such opposing views, she might consider a relationship. But if he wouldn't move because it was too painful, then was he even over Meghan? Good grief. Here she was contemplating falling for Beckett and he didn't even think of her in a romantic way. He'd never once indicated he was attracted to Aurora. Comfort? Protection? Yes. Could she call those things romantic feelings for her? No.

He was doing his duty. Beckett had as much as told her so and on more than one occasion. She was acting like a schoolgirl. She was no schoolgirl.

What she needed was a good dose of reality, and she wasn't going to get that from a newlywed. She placed her coffee cup in the tub by the door and walked across the street to the courthouse to talk to Kelly. If anyone would give it to her straight, it was the judge.

She ignored gawks from people hanging around the square, people still angry with her for defending Austin Bledsoe, and entered the courthouse, the smell of wood polish and something spicy smacking her senses. She strolled down the corridor to Kelly's chambers, knocked and waited.

No answer. She wouldn't be in court this late in the afternoon. Aurora turned the knob and cracked the door. "Kelly?" She pushed it open and froze, blood whooshing in her ears and her head whirling.

Kelly slumped in her leather chair, head lolling to the side.

No. *No.*

Something caught her eye; she blinked to make sure she was seeing straight. The room tilted. On the wall behind Kelly, the words *Aurora Daniels Is Guilty* had been spray-painted. She hoped it was spray paint. It was in bold red letters.

She grappled for oxygen but forced herself to rush to Kelly's limp side. She checked her pulse, though she knew it was too late.

Kelly was dead. A brand-new grandmother. An important judge. Her mentor. The whole reason she'd come to Hope.

And Aurora was to blame.

Who could have gotten in here? Same man

who'd gotten into her office. Beckett had said he hadn't splintered the wood like at her home, but it could still be one and the same man. How could no one have seen him?

And once he got inside, why hadn't Kelly hit the security button under her desk to call a bailiff? Had she been blindsided? Had she known her attacker? If it had been Trevor Russell or another local citizen, she might have trusted them.

Aurora fumbled for her phone and dialed the only person she did trust.

Beckett.

He answered on the second ring. "Counselor. The judge good with you spending a few nights with her?"

Aurora closed her eyes, pushing back the burning tears threatening to spill down her cheeks. "Beckett." Her voice cracked.

"What's wrong?"

"Kelly's—Kelly's dead." She covered her mouth and turned away from the sight.

"I'm pulling up to the courthouse now." The line went dead and before she'd stumbled all the way to the door, Beckett bounded inside and wrapped Aurora in his arms. He stroked her hair and nestled her closer to him, his masculine scent bringing a steady rhythm to her wildly beating heart. "I'm so sorry, Aurora. But this isn't your fault."

"Yes," she muttered into his chest, "it is. She's

dead because of me. Read the writing on the wall. Literally."

Beckett heaved a sigh and put a foot of distance between them, lifting her chin. "You are not guilty or to blame. I need to call in the crime-scene unit. If you want to get a drink of water or step away, that'll be all right. In fact, you really ought to."

Aurora shook her head. "No, I'd like to stay. I won't impede the investigation."

He massaged a scruffy cheek. "I have to call a deputy in. I know you want to stay, but we don't need to be here alone."

She nodded. "Yes, of course. You're right. Anyone could say I tampered with evidence. Call in the deputy. Let him log who comes in and out."

"And I need to call the coroner," Beckett murmured. He made the calls as they stood in the hallway. "We'll have to send what we find through the lab in Memphis. Could take a while, but we won't stop until we find who did this."

"No, we won't." She leaned her head against the concrete wall. "You don't think Trevor Russell could have done this, do you?"

"I wasn't ruling him out with the attacks and phone calls, but to murder Kelly in cold blood…it doesn't feel like something he'd do. But…whoever did this knows you were close to Kelly. Wanted to possibly make you feel the same grieving misery they felt. Trevor does ring that bell."

"Whoever killed Gus McGregor might want me to know I'm guilty for digging into the case. He wants me to stop while I'm ahead or more people will die." Aurora couldn't quit. Not now. More than ever her brother needed vindication, and Kelly's murderer needed to be brought to justice. "I need to call Kelly's son." Once again someone was dead because of her. And there was no running away this time.

FIVE

Beckett didn't know what to say to make Aurora's pain go away. To make her see this wasn't her fault. He knew better than anyone you couldn't change a person's mind or heart from believing what it wanted. The terror and sorrow pulsing from her eyes seared into his chest. He now had two cases that involved Aurora—finding who had targeted her and who had killed Judge Kelly Marks. His gut screamed they were one and the same.

The coroner arrived, along with one of Beckett's deputies and two techs.

"Can you tell me the cause of death?" Due to bruising around the neck area, Beckett suspected strangulation.

James Wheaton, a man in his sixties, examined Kelly and backed up Beckett's suspicions. "I'll know more once we get her to the morgue."

Aurora flinched as they claimed Kelly's body. Outside, a crowd had already congregated. News media snapped photos. Someone must have heard the call on the scanner or leaked it. The thought that one of his own people might be sharing confidential information—like the brand of whiskey Austin Bledsoe had been drinking—sent a wave of nausea through him.

Beckett worked with the county crime techs. While they photographed and dusted for prints, he riffled through Kelly's office drawers and day planner. He placed several items into evidence bags. Aurora might recognize anything out of the ordinary. Someone had broken in and managed to kill Judge Marks without anyone hearing and without a struggle. Other than a few papers on the floor, it appeared Kelly had let the murderer walk in and kill her. Which brought his next thought. Had Kelly been murdered, then staged in the chair? If he was in the room when she came in the door, he could have been behind it and gotten the jump on her, then placed her in the chair and painted the walls. It was too red to be blood, and Kelly, from all appearances, had no other injuries. It was times like this he wished they'd had security cameras at the courthouse. But that was small towns. No one expected something like this to happen.

Aurora sat on a wooden bench in the hall.

"Did you call Kelly's son?"

"Yes. He's on his way." She stretched her neck as she massaged it.

"What did you tell him?" He set the evidence box down and nestled beside her.

"That I found her dead in her chambers. Homicide. And that it could relate to my brother's case or a case I handled recently." Her phone rang and Beckett peeped at the screen. Oliver Benard. Benard. He was one of her previous colleagues at the Chicago law firm. Was that the man who'd been calling and she'd been avoiding?

"Might ought to answer."

Aurora switched her phone to decline and resumed resting her head on the wall. "Kelly's son says it could connect to one of her cases I tried and lost. But I know that's not true, and when it comes to light, he'll hate me. It's my fault his newborn baby won't know her grandmother."

Against his better judgment, he loosed the cell from her hand and enveloped her fingers in his. She didn't pull away and that set off a new sensation. One that shouldn't be going off. Especially now. He was only comforting her. But that one acceptance comforted him. "If you were a client on trial, what would you use as the defense?"

Aurora rubbed her temple with her free hand, but continued to let him hold on to her other. "I'd tell the jury that I couldn't be held responsible for someone else's actions."

"Then you need to accept your own representation. For once, you're right."

Aurora opened one eye and slid him a glance. "Kelly was my only constant."

An urge to proclaim he'd be a constant in her life threatened to slip from his mouth, but he forced it down. "Let's get you to the inn. You could use some rest, and then we can grab some dinner and if you feel up to it, go through this box of stuff I retrieved from her chambers."

"You want me to go through possible evidence?"

"Do you plan on defending the man who did it?"

A scowl answered his rhetorical question.

"It's not like you're investigating, Aurora. You're going through a good friend's effects. And if something pops, you tell me and I'll handle the investigating. It won't mess with the case. It's no different than if I put together a lineup and you identified an attacker. Basically, if you see something odd, you're pointing the finger at a suspect in the lineup."

"That's a stretch, Sheriff, and you know it. But I'll buy it. And...if I need to find a way around something—legally, of course—I'll do it."

It was further than he had expected to get. "Good."

"I want to be at the coroner's office when her

son gets into town. I need to be available to help him with arrangements." Aurora stood, letting her hand slip free from Beckett's.

"I'll come, too. Whatever he needs, we'll make sure he gets." He collected the box and led Aurora to the Tahoe, then proceeded to the inn. Inside, it was quiet, and the smell of something sweet reminded Beckett he was starving. "I'll get us rooms for a few more nights. I didn't think…" She was supposed to be staying with Kelly.

Aurora slipped her upper lip between her teeth and blinked rapidly. "This is a public place. Do you honestly think you need to stay next door to me?"

"I won't bother you tonight unless…unless you need me." What a tough pill to swallow. He wanted Aurora Daniels to need him. He needed to be needed. But she had to process. To grieve. Alone.

"You're not a bother. I just hate dragging you into this. I…" Consideration beamed from her eyes. "I don't want you to get hurt."

She was worried about his safety when she was the vulnerable one. "Counselor, don't worry about me. I'm a big boy and can take care of myself." He inched closer. "And I can take care of you, too," he murmured and hoped for all it was worth that his words were true. He'd failed before.

A tear trickled down her cheek, and she brushed

it away before he could. Probably best. He had no business wiping away her tears, touching her in any kind of tender manner. She was off-limits.

"How about we order room service? I'll have it delivered to my room and bring you yours." He wasn't taking chances. Aurora wasn't opening her door to anyone but him. Period. End of story.

"I'm not hungry."

"You need to eat."

"All right. But only because I'm too tired to argue with you."

"You? Too tired to argue?" He lifted an eyebrow, hoping for a smile. A small one, even. She responded with an unamused pout. "Stay here. I'll go get the rooms."

"I'm also too tired to point out you're ordering me around again." She blew a stray strand of hair from her face.

He chuckled. "Yes, I can see how you're not pointing that out. Sit tight." Before she had the chance to object he raised his hands. "That was a suggestion not a command."

"Doubt that," Aurora called as he met Keeley McKay at the reception desk, her hair hanging around her collarbone and curious eyes locked on his. Great. He'd gotten the gossipy sister.

"Hey, Sheriff. I saw that you and the defense attorney spent the night here—"

"Separate rooms. There's nothing romantic

about this." Beckett made sure to keep his gaze cool and his voice firm. He didn't need either of their reputations sullied. He wasn't exactly sure where Aurora stood with the Lord, but he'd seen her at church a handful of times and she'd attended a few events with Blair. Either way, Beckett wouldn't let the town think ill of her. Or him.

"Oh, I know that!" She gave a subtle laugh. "I don't see the sheriff and the local defense attorney hooking up."

"No one is hooking up regardless of our occupations."

"I meant forging a relationship." She waved off the notion as if it were the most ridiculous thing on the planet. And it was. Still curdled in his gut.

"Poor Judge Marks. Terrible. Is someone after Miss Daniels? I heard about her car getting keyed and that you made a trip over to Trevor Russell's. I can't help but think if she'd have let that boy be tried as an adult this might not have happened. I mean he's not twelve, you know?"

Keeley only echoed what most folks were thinking. What he'd thought. "Well, what's done is done. I'd appreciate it if you didn't advertise us staying here."

"Are the guests safe with her being here? I mean if someone is trying to hurt her."

"Yes. Best not to alert them and cause a panic, though. It'll be our secret."

She seemed to enjoy that. "Well, okay then. I can keep a secret."

Doubtful. "I'm not sure how many more nights we need. Can you book us for the week? And if anyone comes in wanting our room numbers, you call me immediately and don't give them out."

"I won't." She gestured to Aurora. "It's just all so terrible."

Beckett accepted the key cards. "Yes, it is." He strode back to Aurora. "We're all set indefinitely. Let's go up." He led Aurora up the stairs and paused at her door. "I'm going to go in first. Do a precautionary check, then you can peruse the menu."

She stood outside the door while he slid his key card in the lock and entered. Nothing out of place. No one lurking. "Come on in."

Aurora strode inside and toed off her shoes and socks, then rubbed her upper arms.

Beckett bumped up the heat and grabbed the menu off the cherrywood writing desk. He handed it to her and waited. She rolled her eyes and perched on the edge of the bed, flipping open the leather-bound menu. "I guess I'll go with the tomato-basil soup and the grilled Gouda cheese sandwich on wheat." She closed the menu with a dramatic snap. "Happy?"

"Ecstatic." He ignored her huffing and puffing, like she was about to blow her top any second. He marched to the phone and ordered her dinner and for himself a grilled salmon po'boy with a side salad and a bowl of tomato-basil soup. And two orders of chocolate mousse.

"I didn't say I wanted dessert. What if I don't even like chocolate? You assume, Mr. Take Charge." Irritated. Cute.

"But I do know you like chocolate. I suppose I could have asked. You would have turned it down, though. You need to fatten up anyway."

"So now I'm too skinny and stupid to order what I want?" She stood and eyed him. "I call my own shots."

She was gearing up to unload on him. The tone was unmistakable. He couldn't help himself and cracked a grin. "Yes, ma'am."

"This is not for your amusement."

Beckett had seen wet hens less angry. "No, I see it's not." He wasn't so sure Aurora was fired up at him, but in general. She'd had more trauma than one person deserved in a short amount of time. And, he had to admit, she'd been holding it together better than most grown men. All that pent-up emotion was bound to erupt. But Aurora wasn't the kind of woman to fall apart at the seams, and he marveled at that. No, sir, he wouldn't have to pick her up off the floor and put the pieces back together—not that he wouldn't, and be 100 percent fine with it if she did break—but Aurora had gumption.

She chose to fight instead of cry. Aurora Daniels was born a fighter, and not just in a courtroom. So he let her unload on him. He understood her need and was discovering each day he enjoyed and wanted to be her sounding board.

"And instead of babysitting me, you could be out there catching a killer." She narrowed her eyes.

He inhaled, ready for the mudslinging to commence. *Go ahead, Aurora. Get it out.*

"I don't trust any of your Barney Fifes! Law enforcement always fails. First Richie, now Kelly." She stomped across the small room, hands flailing. "You should train your people properly. Do more extensive background checks. Pay better or something to get sufficient help." Up and down the carpet, she wore a path, ranting about his sheriff's department and its incompetence, her voice pronouncing each word with precision as she made her case, as if these were closing arguments.

Beckett stood statuesque while she channeled all her pent-up anger into him.

"And you! You're the worst of them all."

This was getting interesting. He braced himself, ready for her to go for the jugular. Any second—

"You see a criminal in every person that walks the street. You have no mercy. No compassion! You're a muscled machine..."

Her words flailed fast and furious. No compassion? No mercy? The vulnerable side of him flinched at the barb. He reminded himself she was spouting angry words. She didn't mean them.

Did she?

"You don't think I'm compassionate?" He blocked her warpath, unable to contain himself, and she bumped straight into his chest. She raised her head.

"No. I think you think you're the judge and the jury. Like you're God or something. You're not. If it was up to you, you'd lock up boys like Austin Bledsoe, throw away the key and never look back!"

That pumped the heat in his blood up a few degrees. "You mean boys who murder people because they've broken the law? Boys who rob families and communities of loved ones? Those boys?"

"I'm not saying he shouldn't be punished, but you can't throw him away! You can't throw Richie away!" she shouted as a sob hiccupped from her lips.

Sympathy for her grieving state cooled his temper. Maybe she meant it. Maybe not. Either way, she was seeing nothing but her deceased brother and being fueled by despair. "Austin," Beckett whispered. "Not Richie."

Her cloudy blues cleared and widened. She

clamped her hands over her mouth, as if registering she'd crossed a few lines.

A knock sounded through the adjoining room. "Our food's here." He left her to grab their dinner, though he'd lost some of his appetite. But if he didn't eat, he knew she wouldn't, and she needed it more than he did. The woman couldn't live off coffee and poached eggs. He pushed the cart to her room.

An empty room.

"Counselor?"

"I'm in the bathroom. Do I need permission for that, too?"

He sighed. Guess she still had some hissy fit left in her. After removing the lids to the trays, he arranged them at the table for two next to the window. Gave it a second thought and moved the table to the corner of the room. Away from an open shot.

She crept from the bathroom. "I'm terribly sorry. I shouldn't have said those things."

"It's no skin off my teeth." He'd already forgiven her. "Everyone's entitled to come apart."

"It's objectionable."

"You're upset." He gestured to the food, hoping she'd allow him to let her off the hook.

"I'm losing my mind if I can be honest."

"I'd say you've been pretty honest."

Her cheeks colored. "Again, I'm sorry."

"Like I said, you're upset, angry…"

"But that doesn't mean I can verbally beat you up when all you've done is work to protect me. And show me compassion," she added gingerly, settling in front of the chair. Beckett scooted it to the table, then sat across from her as she laid a white linen napkin on her lap.

"Well, it's the only way you could beat me up," he teased. "I am just a muscled machine," he said, hoping to lighten the atmosphere.

She plunged her spoon into her soup and paused. "I didn't say that."

"Oh, you did." He took a healthy bite of his sandwich and wiped the corner of his mouth. "Memory of an elephant, remember?"

She guffawed, then took a bite of her sandwich, her stomach growling.

"I knew you were hungry."

Sighing, she ignored him and they ate in uncomfortable silence. Half a sandwich later, she pushed her plate away. "I'd like to go through Kelly's things."

"You should rest."

"Beckett." The way she said his name. A plea. A question. Hopeful eyes bored into his.

"Fine. I'll roll the rest of your food and dessert outside."

Aurora grabbed the mousse cup. "It's here now. No point in it going to waste."

"Mmm-hmm."

"How do you know I like chocolate? You said you knew I did."

If he told her that he'd smelled it on her earlier, it might come across creepier than it was. "Good guess."

"Mmm-mmm." She scooped a mountainous bite and closed her eyes. "Great guess," she said with satisfaction. He chuckled and rolled the cart outside, but something she'd said had struck a chord. Did he think he was God? Not in a literal sense, of course. He knew he was only a man. Flawed and bone and flesh. But when it came to work, was he only being an agent of justice or was he indeed trying to act as judge and jury? He'd almost put to death the man who had murdered his fiancée. He hadn't seen himself as a judge but emotionally outraged, which had sent him spiraling into a dark place. Terrified him.

But now...

It needled him, but he shrugged it aside and focused on the strawberry blonde finally showing signs of easing into relaxation.

Aurora Daniels. Tough. Shrewd. And a chocoholic. Whatever was he going to do with her? What was he going to do about these crazy feelings cropping up?

* * *

Aurora finished her mousse, and, though she'd never admit it to Beckett, it'd hit the spot. While she was still emotionally exhausted and—if she was being honest—spiritually exhausted, too, she'd had a burst of physical energy and was ready to comb through Kelly's personal items, which Beckett had brought with him.

She'd pummeled Beckett, and shame crept into her cheeks. What right did she have to act spoiled like that? To take out her hurt on him? But he'd let her. He'd stood there quiet, tender yet strong and towering while she sliced him with her words about his department…about him personally. Only when she'd dinged his compassion had he shown any signs of prickled skin.

He'd shown her as much compassion in the last three days as anyone in her entire life had. Beckett the law enforcer wasn't the same as Beckett the man. Or was he? He'd been protecting her, doing due diligence as sheriff.

A man had taken the life of his greatest love, right before they were supposed to spend forever on earth together. Aurora was nothing short of callous. Insensitive. Where was her compassion?

"Counselor?" Beckett called from across the room, a cardboard box in his arms. "Everything all right?"

No. Nothing was right. Aurora wasn't sure anything would be right again, but she had to buck up, pull up her proverbial bootstraps. "I'm fine." Just feeling terrible about how she'd been treating him. A man who'd been wounded. No wonder he was swift to stamp *guilty* on every person he put cuffs on. He'd seen evil up close and personal. His future had been ripped out from under him at the hands of a vicious killer.

What about Aurora? She was equally guilty, but Beckett hadn't condemned her. Instead, he'd reminded her she was innocent, without blame. If only that were true.

He laid the box on the edge of the bed. He'd showered and his short-cropped walnut-colored hair had curled, his five-o'clock shadow adding mystery to him and emphasizing his thick lips. She tried to ignore the way his flannel shirtsleeves were rolled to the elbows, exposing muscled forearms under his naturally olive skin, and what it did to her pulse. She fought off the urge to stare, to drool like an infatuated teenager.

"I've been thinking about how it all happened. Someone Kelly knew must have been her killer. How else would he have gotten inside so easily?" Aurora asked. "She would have screamed. Called for help." Better to stay focused on the task at hand. But when he closed the distance between them, his fresh shower scent clouded her senses.

Beckett pinched the bridge of his nose. "Not necessarily. Not if the killer had any kind of military experience. I could easily have done it. If he'd caught her off guard or moved fast, with a certain hold she wouldn't have had the ability to scream, and if he'd used a technique to knock her out first—a maneuver to a pressure point—it would have been silent. Quick. Painless."

Aurora dropped her jaw.

Beckett winced. "I didn't mean to give you a visual, but it is possible. With her office being on the ground floor, he could have come through a window and been waiting for her."

"Like at my house."

"Right. He could have done the unlocking in the middle of the night. Who checks their windows in the morning? Then he came back later and it would have been easy to raise it without being heard."

Aurora pawed her face, the horrific visions of Kelly's last moments plaguing her to nausea. She gulped, then plunged a shaky hand into the box, retrieving a leather daily planner and opening it. "Did you get her phone?"

Beckett pulled out a plastic evidence bag. "Yeah. You know the password?"

"Try Hotty Toddy."

"Serious? An Ole Miss chant?"

"Chant. Cheer. Greeting. She was serious about

the Rebels." Aurora flipped to this week's dates. Kelly had the best handwriting. She paused. "That's odd."

"What is it?" Beckett had Kelly's phone in hand. Guess he wasn't too worried about his prints ending up on it. But latex gloves wouldn't work on the touch screen. "And I'm in."

Aurora wasn't sure it was anything other than strange. "She had an appointment with Oliver Benard. He's the—"

"Partner at your old firm in Chicago, and the number you're avoiding on your phone. Does he have personal ties to Kelly?"

Aurora sat stunned. "You know all this? I'm not sure if I should be frightened or relieved." She shook her head. "How are you aware of all this?"

"I did a check because it's what I do. It's who I am. And I noticed his name pop up on one of those unanswered calls. So…" He shrugged. "Did he know Kelly, too?"

"No. I mean, he knew I had a mentor and that she lived here. But, as far as a personal relationship, no." Why would she have an appointment with Oliver?

"When was the appointment?" Beckett asked.

"Yesterday."

Beckett scrolled through Kelly's phone. "Several calls from Oliver Benard over the past week. What time was the appointment?"

"Eleven a.m. Doesn't say where. Any calls from him after that?"

Beckett scanned the phone. "No. Did she have court cases after that time?"

"No." Had the killer known that? No one would come looking for her in her chambers if she wasn't expected in court. "I wonder if Kelly showed for that appointment and it got her killed."

"If Oliver is behind this, he had time to follow us, cut the chain, drive back to Richfield for his appointment and kill Kelly." Beckett put the phone away.

But why would Oliver Benard want to kill Kelly? What could she possibly know or say that would lead him to murder her. "I should have answered his calls." She might have been able to stop him if he'd had something to do with Kelly's death. Another sharp stab of guilt gouged her ribs, grinding and cutting.

"Did she mention him at all?" Beckett asked.

"Only to tell me to answer his calls. That he might be extending me some grace." Aurora closed the planner.

"Is there any other reason he might be calling you now?"

"His son was murdered on February fifteenth, two years ago. That's a little over a week away."

Beckett's eyes turned to slits. "I don't like it. I'm not saying he couldn't be calling to offer you grace. But more than likely, he wants to get close to you."

Aurora swallowed.

Close enough to kill?

SIX

It was Monday morning and Aurora's gloves, coat and scarf weren't enough to keep out the cold front in her bones since Kelly's death on Friday.

She sat in the passenger seat of Beckett's Tahoe. He was taking her home to retrieve more clothing and toiletries. He'd been on her like white on snow all weekend as they worked through the case. Turned out the writing on the wall in Kelly's chambers had been spray paint. And the only thing Aurora noted missing was a wooden gavel she'd given Kelly as a Christmas present that sat on her desk, but she could have taken it home.

Beckett had tried to question Trevor Russell, but Trevor's father said he was out of town. Needed some space. Seemed a little convenient.

Aurora had met with Kelly's son on Saturday and helped him make arrangements for the funeral, which was taking place tomorrow morning.

Beckett cranked up the heat in his Tahoe. They'd left The Black-Eyed Pea, where, in his typical demanding way, Beckett had forced Aurora to eat something, but Aurora didn't have the fight to complain. She'd choked down half a hot, open-faced roast beef sandwich and a cup of vegetable soup. Which seemed to satisfy Beckett enough that he didn't order a dessert.

"Cold?" he asked.

No amount of heat would shake off the chill. "I'll be fine."

"I've been thinking. It might be best not to call Oliver Benard. If you've declined his calls this long, it would seem suspicious you calling now."

Aurora rubbed the edges of her scarf between her fingers. "I don't know why he was calling, but Oliver wouldn't murder Kelly."

Beckett turned left on Maplewood.

"Where are we going?" Aurora asked. "I thought you were taking me home."

Beckett undid a butterscotch wrapper with his teeth and popped it in his mouth. "So, my mom heard about Judge Marks. And she knows you and she are tight…"

"Okaaay."

"She made you chocolate muffins."

"Ha! I knew it." She lightly pounded her fist on her thigh in victory.

Beckett crinkled his nose. "Knew what?"

"You didn't force me to eat dessert. Now I know why."

Beckett grimaced. "I don't *force* you to do anything."

"'Eat your eggs.' 'Eat your soup before it gets cold.' 'We're not leaving until you eat.' 'Get in the car.' 'Sit down.' 'Stay here.' I'm not sure if you see me as a person or a pet." She was half joking, but she'd never met anyone so commanding.

Beckett turned into a small graveled drive that led to a cozy, cottage-style home. He turned off the engine and directed his attention to Aurora. "One, I want you to keep your strength up, and you haven't been eating enough. Soldiers who don't eat get weak. They fall behind. They make poor or rash decisions—"

"I'm not a soldier. I'm a defense attorney." She held his gaze.

"Not right now. You're in a war, Counselor. As bad as I hate to say it, an enemy is after you and it's scary. I know you feel a heavy weight on your shoulders, and I'm trying my best to help you carry it. I don't have time for pretty prose."

"You think using considerate words is pretty prose? Ha!" But Aurora's heart tripped at the words he'd used before that remark. Part fear, part something she didn't want to pinpoint or deal with. Long ago, she'd heard a preacher say Jesus wanted to carry her burdens. She'd never figured out how to transfer them from her shoulders to His, so eventually she'd stopped trying. Beckett was right. She did feel a heavy weight. "I appreciate all your help. And your mom's muffins."

"Which you'll eat."

She glared. "Pretty prose, please."

He graced her with a killer smile. "Which I hope you'll eat."

Aurora wanted to fan herself. In winter. It wasn't lack of food that might send her into making a rash or poor decision. It was Beckett Marsh's grin. Mercy, it was billboard worthy. "I will."

At the front stoop, he turned the knob and opened the door, but before they went inside he gently caught her arm, bringing her back against his chest, the scent of spice and pine swirling through her senses. He pressed his mouth to her ear, close enough for his breath to tickle her neck. "When I see you, Counselor, the last thing I see is a pet. I promise you that." His voice had turned husky, tickling her side. What did he see?

Her throat dried out, and she refused to ask for fear she might like the answer entirely too much for her own good.

"Beck! Is that you?" A sweet voice filled the air, along with cocoa and cinnamon. Already, Aurora adored Mrs. Marsh.

She might adore her son a little more than she should, too.

Beckett's mom came into view. Aurora had never officially met her, but she'd seen her at church the handful of times Aurora had gone. Tall and slender, Virginia Marsh shared her son's eyes: amber irises with thick, ebony limbal rings rimming them. Her hair had a few streaks of gray and was a bit darker brown than Beckett's. Her lips weren't as plump and her teeth weren't as straight. But she was a striking woman.

"Miss Daniels, it's a pleasure. Please come in. I was so sorry to hear about Judge Marks. She was such a sweet woman. Let me take your coat, hon."

"Thank you."

Beckett helped her shrug out of her coat, and she tried not to tremor when his warm hand reached the small of her back and guided her into the kitchen toward the smell of coffee and muffins as big as his fist. "Oh, those look fantastic."

"They're my specialty, and Beckett said you were a big fan of chocolate." She gave him a sideways glance, and he turned his head and rubbed his ear. Aurora found it adorable.

"I mentioned I thought you might like chocolate," Beckett mumbled, and pulled out a chair for Aurora. "Cream and sugar in your coffee?"

Virginia blinked deliberately a few times. "You might ask her if she wants some first?"

Beckett huffed like a child being scolded and turned to Aurora. "You want coffee, Counselor?"

She almost said no to ruffle his feathers but, instead, nodded. "Cream and sugar since it's clear you're going to fix it for me."

"You want to pour your own cup?" Impatience lined his face and Aurora relished the moment. Getting under his skin. Seeing him squirm. A tough guy with a mama's boy's heart. Oh, what it did to hers.

"No. I think I'll sit right here and tell you how to do it."

His rich eyebrows slowly stretched upward, and if she wasn't so sensible, she might think his gaze held a measure of flirtation.

Mrs. Marsh chuckled and brought the tray of muffins to the table. Aurora helped herself to one, still warm. Decadent. Delicious. "These are wonderful."

"Take them with you—they make your whole house smell good." She handed Aurora a napkin.

"My whole house? I'm—"

"Gonna down them before she gets the chance to use them as potpourri, Mama." Beckett gave her the eye, and Aurora refrained from finishing her thought. Beckett didn't want his mother to know about the threats, that Aurora was in danger, therefore putting Beckett in danger, as well. Protecting his mother from worry.

"He's right about me eating them before we ever make it to the car. I can eat a lot."

Beckett snorted. "You need to eat more."

She ignored him and focused on Mrs. Marsh. "You have a lovely home." Worn. Certainly dated from the late eighties, but the atmosphere felt like love. Like home. Like a place ought to. Unlike the house she had been raised in. A house and a home were two different things. Beckett's dad may have left them and they might have struggled financially, but he'd had something Aurora hadn't. A home.

Beckett eased into a seat at the table.

Mrs. Marsh beamed. "Thank you. Now that I'm retired, all I have to do is tidy the place. But I've lived here my whole life. Can't imagine going anywhere else. Plus, it's nice having Beck home and close."

"Mama, you're being modest." He grabbed a muffin. "Mama works for the homeless shelter in downtown Memphis twice a week, and she's helping the Women's Club with the Valentine's Dinner and Dance to raise money for St. Jude."

Nothing short of respect and admiration danced over Beckett's face. He was proud of his mother, as he should be. Aurora had never been proud of hers. Another slice of shame to add to her list. She sipped her coffee. "I need you at the café, Mrs. Marsh. This is great coffee."

"Virginia, hon. Call me Virginia. And thank you."

"Virginia." Aurora noticed photos of Beckett on

the picture ladder leaning on the wall in the dining room. Handsome in his navy uniform.

Virginia followed the direction of her sight. "I don't think I've ever had to trust God more than when Beck was in the navy, the SEALs. Never knowing where he was or if he was in one piece. Gone for nine months to a year sometimes. Like I said, it's nice having him home and safe. All this gray hair—" she pointed to her head "—from Beck and his dangerous missions. A mama worries."

"That must have been difficult and, yet, how proud you must be to have such a brave, giving son to dedicate his life to keeping others safe." Aurora checked out Beckett, who was paying more attention than necessary to his muffin. Compliments must be tough for him to handle. But he was brave and self-sacrificing. If she kept going down this line of thinking, she'd faint dead out of her chair.

"I am very proud. It's also nice to not fret. I'm getting too old for that." She laughed.

Beckett patted her hand. "Mama, don't worry. I'm not going anywhere."

Aurora caught the flash of something in his eyes. Was he thinking about Wilder's offer? She switched topics. "So, how are things going with the Valentine's Day Dinner and Dance? I've never been, but I always donate. St. Jude does so much for children."

The strain in the room calmed.

"Oh, it's good. It'll be at Mitch Rydell's again. In that big ol' barn of his. It's heated out there—did you know that?"

"No." Aurora shook her head. "I've only been to Mitch's twice. Dinner. Not held in his barn."

"You had dinner with Mitch Rydell?" Beckett's voice deepened and he held her with what would be an intimidating stare—if Beckett intimidated her.

"Twice. Not in the barn." She smirked. "In case you didn't hear me the first time."

Virginia pressed her lips together, amusement twinkling in her eyes. "I'm gonna top off my cup." She excused herself. Beckett continued to pin Aurora with a daggered look.

"What? I'm single. He's single. And he's a nice guy." Not that she had any interest in Mitch. He was a handsome man, but Aurora wasn't interested in a romantic relationship. And she and Mitch didn't have chemistry.

Unlike the chemistry that popped and sizzled around Beckett. Chemistry that couldn't be acted upon.

Beckett tossed his arm carelessly behind his chair, reclining. "I don't care who you have dinner with. I just don't see the two of you happening."

"Well," she mused, "I didn't say we were happening. I said I had dinner with him." No dessert, now that she thought about it. Unlike Beckett—who shoved a sweet down her after every meal.

Virginia returned. "You asked about the dance. It's going to be a big hit. Each ticket is fifty dollars, but you can donate more. You should come to this one."

"Maybe Mitch will ask you," Beckett muttered.

Aurora squinted. Was Beckett Marsh jealous of Mitch? "Maybe he will." And she'd say no. Like last year. "Are *you* going?"

"I go every year. Civic duty and all that mess." He shrugged. Who was he taking as his date? He stood. "We gotta go, Mama." He leaned over and pecked her cheek. "See you soon."

Virginia walked them to the door, making sure Aurora took the muffins. "I have some paperwork to do," Beckett said as they got in the car.

"Can we run by my house and grab some clothes and toiletries first?"

He nodded, suddenly in a surly mood. They drove in silence to her home. She missed her own bed. Her own shower. They entered, Beckett first, and she started to her room.

"Stop," he commanded.

She was exhausted, but she turned on her heel. "What?"

"Where do you think you're going?" He pushed past her. "I haven't even cleared the bedroom."

She'd argue over his gruff commands if he

wasn't right. After what had happened to Kelly... She shuddered. "Fine, but diplomacy is a real thing. Invest in it."

He cracked a smile, then gestured with his chin to back up. She acquiesced and gave him the "are you happy?" snarl.

He pushed the door open with his foot and raised his weapon, sending a flood of panic through her. "Stay," he demanded, and disappeared into Aurora's bedroom.

She waited anxiously until he came into the hall.

"Well? What's wrong?"

Tight-lipped and scowling, he hesitantly motioned for her. "Come inside."

Aurora's room had been ransacked. Clothes were strewn all over. That's when she noticed it.

Beckett, too. He picked up one of her navy blue power suits.

It had been shredded.

Like all her clothes that had been hanging in the closet.

Beckett scanned the room as he held Aurora's blue suit. He'd seen her wear it in court often. The dark blue contrasted nicely with the powder blue of her eyes. Her sweet scent still lingered on the slashed material. He laid it on the bed and stalked to the closet. Everything had been sliced, most pieces tossed around the room in disarray. A few articles were barely hanging on satiny hangers. Aurora Daniels *would* use plush, satiny hangers.

He stormed from the closet and jerked open a drawer on a tall, skinny chest.

"Hey!" she shouted.

Undergarments.

Heat flushed his cheeks. "Sorry." He slammed the drawer shut. "Check the drawers, see if anything else has been shredded."

He gave her some privacy as she methodically searched through her chest of drawers and dresser. "Only my suits and dress clothes." She tapped the tip of her nose and stared into the dark closet.

"What are you thinking?"

Aurora scratched the base of her neck, under the tight bun she wore consistently. "My suits define me. When I'm in them, I'm an attorney. I have a task to do. Someone doesn't like my job. Who I am. So they destroyed them."

Perceptive. Smart. Great point. "I think you're right. Let's check the rest of the house. Be sure nothing else has been disrupted or taken. Any clothing missing?" Meghan had noticed a few items from her personal drawers missing, but she'd chalked it up to losing them at the Laundromat. He should have caught on to something sinister then. He wouldn't make that mistake this time. "Double-check your girlie drawers."

"My girlie drawers?" Aurora rolled her eyes and grumbled something about men, then did a recheck. "Nothing is missing."

A small amount of relief filled him, but not taking personal items didn't mean she wasn't in grave danger.

She was.

Bounding into the hall and toward the living room, Beckett said, "You think whoever killed Gus McGregor did this? It could have been—and I hate to say it—Trevor Russell. Or whoever chucked that Old Crow whiskey bottle through your window. Trevor could have done both."

"I thought the same thing on all accounts." She picked at her thumbnail. "I need to pack a bag. I have a couple suits at the inn. I can make do."

Beckett sat on the couch and massaged his neck. She pointed to the kitchen. "Feel free to grab a soft drink or something."

She padded down the hall and her door clicked shut. Beckett surveyed the house. He wasn't thirsty, but he was curious. He proceeded to the kitchen and nosed through her refrigerator and cabinets until his phone rang.

Wilder.

He growled and declined the call.

"I'm ready when you're done snooping around." Aurora stood in the kitchen doorway, an amused expression on her face. Busted.

"I was curious."

"About my food choices?"

About her in general. He wished he wasn't, but Aurora was a beautiful mystery, and he had always been fascinated by a good mystery. Chuckling, he took her bag and nodded toward the door. "You're quite the healthy eater. Minus the chocolate-filled pantry."

"Which reminds me…" She beelined it to the pantry and grabbed a few junk-food items. "I like to snack when I'm thinking."

"Then how do you stay fit? Because you're always thinking." He swept his gaze over her figure, working not to linger too long, but he could if he let himself, and it drove him crazy. Let her have dinners with Mitch Rydell. What did Beckett care? It'd surely be less complicated if she were with Mitch. Beckett and Aurora were like oil and water. But the jealousy that rose up when he heard that Aurora had shared dinner with Mitch—at Mitch's place—nearly consumed him. It had been so long since he'd had fierce feelings for someone.

He'd always have a love for Meghan, but the way he was feeling about Aurora—and this fast—terrified him. They drove back to the inn without any conversation. Aurora was probably trying to figure out who had wrecked her bedroom and shredded her clothing while Beckett struggled to overcome these emotions stirring up inside him. At the inn, he carried her bags inside.

Beckett's phone rang again.

Wilder.

"You ever gonna answer that?" Aurora asked as he declined Wilder's call.

"Yeah, you ever gonna answer that?"

Beckett swiveled to the left as his oldest and dearest friend—whom he'd been dodging—stood from a chair in the lobby, something between irritation and a pout on his face. He held his phone up high and shook it dramatically.

"Wilder."

"Avoider."

Beckett snorted and shook his head as Wilder pulled him into a fast and hard hug, slapping his back and putting some sting on it.

"How long have you been sitting there? How did you know I was even here? Never mind. You talked to Celia." His secretary. She'd met Wilder on a few occasions, and Wilder had a way of sweet-talking a locked door into coughing up who was behind it.

"I had to play dirty." He brushed invisible lint from his shirt pocket and sniffed. "I might have brought her flowers."

"Pitiful flirt."

Wilder set his sights on Aurora and extended his hand. "This loser hasn't introduced me properly. Wilder Flynn. Bachelor at large, but aiming to settle down with a beauty like yourself."

Aurora shook his hand. "Aurora Daniels. Defense attorney. When someone sues you for harassment."

Beckett laughed. Wilder hooted, completely relaxed. But his trip here wasn't for fun. He was on a mission. "You must be the reason Beckett's camping out here. Celia told me you were on protection detail. Those were her exact words, Beck. She didn't tell me why, though." Concern flickered in his grass-green eyes. Was he having flashbacks of Meghan being stalked?

"Come on up and we'll talk and eat some of Aurora's preservative-laced snack foods." Beckett signaled Wilder to the stairs.

Aurora followed Wilder, and Beckett brought up the rear. He unlocked the door to his room and welcomed them inside, dreading the conversation that lay ahead.

"Beckett tells me you two were SEALs together." Aurora slid off her shoes. In his room. The gesture did peculiar things to his gut. Habit for her, but it felt…strange. Good. Wilder noticed, too, and raised a few questions with his eyes. What would Wilder think if he knew Beckett was having feelings for someone other than his sister?

"We were. I've been trying to get this old coot

to come work for me, though I don't know why. He's not very sharp." Wilder collapsed on a paisley-covered wingback chair and leaned his elbows on his knees. "I guess I'm a sucker for brotherhood."

Aurora dug into the bag of items she'd taken from her house. "I admire loyalty. I'll leave my snack food, minus the brownie bites, and let you two talk. Nice meeting you, Wilder."

"I don't want to be sued, so I'll just say nice meeting you, too." He winked and stood as Aurora excused herself. Beckett followed.

"I'll sweep your room first." He didn't ask her to stick around. He was afraid Wilder might pick up on his feelings. After securing her room, he left her and sat across from Wilder.

"She being stalked?"

"Yes and no." Beckett ran his hands through his hair and briefed Wilder on everything.

"She's brave."

Beckett gave a haphazard shrug. "She eats eggs." He chuckled at the inside joke, realizing how much he enjoyed having an inside joke with her.

Wilder rubbed his chin as if contemplating life's greatest secret. "You're falling for her."

"I'm not." But he was terrified that he was.

"Yes, you are, and it's all good. What's not gonna fly is if you let it keep you from coming to work for me. I don't have an explosives man. With so many bomb threats, you'd be a major asset. You'd get to travel, which I know gives you all the tingles."

Beckett wasn't ready for this conversation. "How's Caley?"

Wilder huffed. "Why are you changing the subject and asking about my baby sister?"

Because he didn't know what to do. The offer appealed more than anything, but with the past looming over him—what he'd tried to do to Meghan's killer—and his desire to give Mama the time and security she deserved, he couldn't jump on it. And he did love being sheriff. Loved the town. The people. "Just curious. She still in Florida saving sea turtles?"

Wilder nodded, a strand of coal-black hair slipping into his eyes. He shoved it back. "Quit trying to change the subject. What's holding you back? This attorney? This *defense* attorney?"

Beckett didn't need reminding of that one horrible word between them. "No. You know why I can't. And I can't leave Mama worrying. Not again."

"I get it, Beck. But I think it's a cop-out." He raised a hand. "I'm not here to argue. And I'm not opposed to you and the attorney. No one expects you to pine the rest of your life for Meg. We won't forget her, man. It's why Covenant Crisis Management exists. But you can't stop living."

Is that what Beckett had done? Stopped living? He'd come home and settled into a safe routine where he wouldn't ever lose himself to that darkness that had tormented and provoked him to seek retribution. Had he simply gone on autopilot?

A shriek sounded from next door.

Beckett snapped to attention and bolted for Aurora.

SEVEN

Aurora shrieked again as Beckett and Wilder burst through the door. She held up a manila envelope, her hand shaking uncontrollably.

"What is it?" Beckett demanded.

"A note. And—"

Beckett turned to Wilder. "Stay here. Watch her." He blasted past her and out the inn door.

Aurora stood in the middle of the room, gaping.

Wilder scanned the room, grabbed Aurora's scarf and used it to take the envelope.

"He just left. I didn't even get to tell him what's inside." Aurora shook her head, her mind reeling.

Wilder peeked inside the manila envelope, about the size of a novel, and scowled. "He didn't have time to waste on hearing what the contents were. He's after who left it." He said it as if he'd casually told her his favorite color. No emotion. Didn't he see what was inside? Her knees turned to water, and she crumpled onto the edge of the hotel bed.

The killer knew she was here. He'd been brazen enough to inch the corner of the envelope, containing the note and the bloodstained wooden gavel, under the door so she'd notice it. The same gavel that Kelly had kept on her desk in her chambers. The same one Aurora had given her as a Christmas present last year. Whoever killed Kelly had stolen it from her chambers and was now reiterating his message that Aurora was guilty. But whose blood was on the gavel? She hadn't seen any blood on Kelly. Had someone close to Aurora been killed, someone they hadn't yet found?

Wilder read the note aloud. "'More people are going to die. It will be your fault. You did this.'" He laid the note and envelope on the desk. "This isn't your fault and you didn't do anything to cause it. Remember that."

She laced her fingers and stared at the door. "I need to call my parents." They weren't close, but what if the killer had... She couldn't finish the thought.

Wilder nodded. "We don't know that this is human blood."

"But it is blood, isn't it?" Aurora dug through her purse and grabbed her phone.

"Yes," Wilder said. "I'll be out in the hall. Give you some privacy." He paused, and his voice lulled. "I won't leave you. Not until Beck gets back. You'll be safe."

She didn't know this man, but as she studied his emerald-green eyes, the resolute set of his squared jaw and pursed lips, she believed it. Word for word. "Thank you." He exited and she called her parents. Her mom answered and confirmed they were both home and fine. Without going into too much detail, Aurora made a second or two of small talk and hung up.

Wilder knocked quietly and slipped back inside. "Beck hasn't called, but he's probably out there kicking butt and taking names. It's kind of his way. Move first. Ask questions later." He pointed to the chair by the table. "May I?" Not quite the flirt he was earlier.

"Of course, have a seat."

"Beckett explained what's been going on. I hope that's all right with you." He crossed an ankle over a knee. The chair seemed like a preschooler's seat underneath him. "I admire your tenacity. To seek justice for your brother. I understand. My career— it's a memorial to my sister every day."

The door opened and Beckett entered, frustration in his eyes. "Whoever did it is long gone. No one saw anything. No security cameras. Might get some prints but, since we haven't so far, it's a long shot. The guy is meticulous and careful."

Aurora paced to the window overlooking what would be a gorgeous garden come spring. Now it was brittle and cracked. Much like Aurora's heart.

"Get away from the window, Counselor!" Beckett barked, and lowered the contents of the envelope he'd been examining.

Aurora startled and jumped out of the window's view.

"So he knocked and you opened it? I told you not to open the door. For anyone." Beckett's words came off as menacing as his command to move from the window; his eyebrows pinched, forming creases along his brow.

Aurora thrust a finger his direction. "First of all, I'm sick to death of you telling me what to do or not to do as if I'm a child. Secondly, he didn't knock. He slid the corner of the envelope under the door. I heard it. I waited a beat and then I opened it. Yes. I did. Against your wishes, because I didn't want to interrupt your conversation next door. I was trying to be considerate. And if he had wanted in, he would have gotten in. You would have heard it and come running. No chance for him to get away. So I. Opened. The door."

"He could have pulled you out into the hall. Drugged you. I wouldn't have heard squat, and guess where you'd be, Aurora? Dead. You'd be dead and *once again* it would be my fault! Mine," he bellowed as he shoved a thumb into his chest, then stomped through the adjoining room door and slammed it so hard the pictures on the walls shook.

Wilder clucked his tongue and stood. "Well,

that wasn't awkward at all." He clasped his hands together at his chin. "He's—"

"Thinking of your sister." But Aurora wasn't Meghan, and it wasn't fair to compare them.

"Not so much of her as his perceived failure to save her. She was gone before he could arrive." He pointed at her. "And he's right, whether you want to hear it or not. If this guy wanted you and was good enough, he could have taken you without making a peep. Tossed you in a laundry cart and wheeled you out of here."

"That's a comforting image."

"It's reality, Aurora. Let Beck do what he does best. Why do you think I hound him all the time? Purely selfish. I need him on my team. Be glad he's on yours."

Wilder was right. Beckett was right. It wasn't the smartest decision she'd ever made, and Beckett struggled with guilt. Aurora understood that better than anyone. She hadn't thought about what it would do to him if something happened to her. "I need to go in there and talk to him. Would you mind…?"

"I'll be right here." He scoped out the table. "Eating your snack cakes and brownie bites."

She liked this guy. It was evident he cared for Beckett like a brother. The thought of Beckett leaving Hope sent a blip to her pulse. She laid a hand on the doorknob. "How long will you be in town?"

"One day, maybe two—unless work calls me away." He rummaged through the snacks. "Go in there. His bark is way worse than his bite."

She scoffed. "You don't know me well. I'm not scared of Beckett Marsh's barks *or* bites."

"No," he said, and paused, amused. "I can see you're not, but I suspect he might be scared of you." He thumbed toward Beckett's door.

Aurora knocked, then slid inside Beckett's room. What exactly did Wilder mean by that last statement?

"Beckett?"

He stood with his back facing her, only his profile in her line of sight. His arms were crossed over his chest, pulling his shirt tight enough to see his well-formed back. "We're changing rooms. Immediately."

"Yes, of course." Whatever he wanted. She trusted him. "I shouldn't have opened the door without consulting you. It wasn't an intelligent decision. I apologize."

"You scared me, Aurora. When I'm scared… I get mad." He shifted slightly, his jaw working overtime.

That was twice he'd said her name. Not *counselor*. These past few days, things had gotten personal between them. At least, they had for her.

More than she wanted to admit. "I didn't mean to scare you." She tiptoed across the room, unsure if it was the right move to make, until she was in his personal space, feeling safer by the second.

Someone was coming for her.

Toying with her.

She touched his bicep, and it flexed like boulders jumping under his skin. "I don't know what else to say."

He turned and fixed his eyes on hers. "I find that hard to believe, Counselor."

"You called me Aurora twice." She liked the way he said her name even if he was scared. Angry.

He studied her face until everything inside her shifted and collapsed. No. She could not be spiraling into love with the sheriff.

He trailed his index finger down her cheek, setting off an explosion of feelings. "So I did. You're supposed to be the enemy."

"But I'm not," she murmured. She just saw the law differently from Beckett.

"That's what worries me." He dropped his hand from her cheek and put a measure of distance between them. "I need to get that letter and gavel to the lab. Find out whose or what kind of blood is on it."

It appeared Beckett also knew they could never work—not in a million years—and he was ending something before it began. Which was the smarter move to make. Clearly he had a more level head than she had in the last twelve hours.

"Right. Good."

Disappointment drowned her heart.

Beckett sat in his plush office chair staring at a lukewarm cup of coffee. After attending Kelly Marks's funeral this morning with Aurora and the lunch afterward, he'd spent the rest of the afternoon recapping yesterday's events and giving Aurora some grieving space. He rolled around the significance of giving Aurora a bloody gavel. Could definitely be Trevor. Waiting on the lab results for prints and the type of blood on the gavel was agonizing. He'd stopped in at Trevor Russell's house earlier, too.

According to Trevor's dad, he was back in town but staying at his cabin near Hope Lake. His son, Quent, had been staying with the grandparents. Beckett ruled out Quent for these last escalating events, though he didn't rule him out for throwing that whiskey bottle or keying Aurora's car the day of the motion. Unfortunately, he couldn't rule out Trevor. It was too convenient being out of town with zero alibi. He'd been in the military—army. He had a vast knowledge of vehicles. Even if Beckett couldn't quite make him fit, he kept him in the back of his mind. Which was why he needed to go out to Hope Lake and have a chat. At least to feel Trevor out. See where his head was.

But then it was easy to lie, to hide true feelings.

Much like he'd done when he'd told Wilder he was fine after Meghan had died and her killer roamed scot-free. Beckett had claimed he'd let the process take its course in bringing Parker Hill—Meghan's murderer—to justice. Wilder had assured him things would be handled properly.

It was then Beckett realized he'd lost all of his faith. In justice. In God. It had terrified him but, with that absence, given him the fuel to seek his own vengeance for Meghan's death. He'd stalked the stalker. While Wilder had used other methods of investigating and worked with law enforcement, Beckett had gone off the deep end, becoming obsessed himself.

He blinked out of the dark place. He never wanted to go back there again. He'd asked for God's forgiveness, but he still hadn't reconciled why bad things happened to good people. To him. He promised himself he'd never lie about how he felt again. That he'd keep Wilder in the loop.

And yet he'd already begun once more.

Wilder had called Beckett on his feelings for Aurora and he'd denied them. The thought of Aurora being kidnapped, killed…set off a frenzy. Not because it brought back his feelings for Meghan or losing her. The guilt of being too late to save her? Yes. But not the ache and longing for her that had persisted long after her death.

That was when he knew he was at peace with letting her go. Not the way in which she went, but that she was gone.

And that he was open to love again.

But Aurora Daniels? Could he be falling in love with her? In the short time they'd spent together?

No. No, it wasn't the tight company they'd been keeping these past several days. It was all the prior months of admiring her strength. Her determination. Her confidence. Maybe it wasn't only her occupation that had put Beckett at arm's length all this time but the fact that, deep down, he was aware he could love her. He could easily fall and fall hard, so he'd made her out to be the enemy when really she was a vulnerable woman working to make something she felt wrong right. She'd let her own guilt fuel her passion to defend those who needed defending. Did she get it wrong on occasion?

Yes.

Did Beckett?

Yes. What was he going to do about it now? These feelings. Did she reciprocate a single one? The way she'd touched his arm, sending off a flood of sensations through him yesterday when she'd sincerely apologized. When she'd let him stroke her cheek. When she'd seemed let down as he pulled away.

He sprang from his office chair, grabbed his coat and keys and stomped to his Tahoe. Time to clear his head, and the best way to do that was to ride out to Hope Lake and talk to Trevor. Wilder was keeping vigil over Aurora. Beckett was thankful he'd arrived when he had. Questioning suspects had to be done, and Aurora had no business going with him.

Slowing as he reached the dirt paths that led up to Trevor's cabin, he whispered a prayer. "God, I don't have a clue what I'm doing. I'm still trying to figure out what You're doing. But please. Please don't...don't take Aurora away." The words *from me*, he left off. Because she didn't belong to him, and he wasn't even sure he'd pursue anything. How in the world would they make it work? He'd arrest someone and she'd grab her coffee and kiss Beckett goodbye to run and defend the guy, assuring him she'd be home in time to eat pitiful snack foods and watch crime TV, to which they'd argue the entire time.

He pressed his fingers across his brow, working to relieve tension. No go. He ambled out of the vehicle, noting Trevor's car wasn't anywhere in sight, and crunched dead leaves as he worked his way up to the porch. He knocked and rubbed his hands together for warmth.

No answer.

Beckett peeked inside the two front windows. Dark. Empty.

A sinking feeling formed in Beckett's gut. He suspected Trevor never had been up at his cabin. And his family might be covering for him, whether they knew what he was doing or not. He was family. Family took care of their own.

He dug out his phone and called Wilder. They were at Aurora's office so she could get some work done. See a few clients—criminals—and catch up on paperwork. Beckett listened to Wilder dote on her professionalism and legal mind all the way back into town before he couldn't stand it any longer and cut the conversation short, then checked in at the station. Lab results came in on the gavel. Animal blood.

Clomping up the steps, he entered Aurora's office. The smell of fresh coffee and cinnamon lightened his mood. Wilder sat in the cramped waiting area, phone to his ear. He pointed at the phone and flashed a dramatic eye roll then mouthed, *Caley.*

Beckett nodded and pointed to Aurora's office.

"She's alone," Wilder whispered.

He waltzed down the hall and knocked on Aurora's door. At her invitation to come inside, he opened it. Hair pulled back in a tight bun on her neck, she'd dressed in black pants and a light blue sweater. A bit more casual than he was used to, but then most of her clothes had been shredded. Someone had attacked her identity. Basically, told her to quit her profession, to stop while she was ahead. But Aurora had more tenacity than that.

"How did things go at the cabin?" she asked.

"They didn't," he said as he plopped into the chair across from her desk. He filled her in, including the lab results on the gavel.

"I'm glad it's not human blood, but it's still sadistic."

"Agreed." He studied her organized desk. "What have you been up to?"

Aurora pushed her chair back and crossed her legs. "I just got off the phone with an old friend of Richie's. Got an extended list of suspected names for those poker games. One of them might have had a beef with Gus."

"What's the friend's name?"

"That's confidential. But I can share the list. I say we take another trip to Richfield and have a tête-à-tête with each participant in those games."

Beckett couldn't help the smile. Sometimes her choice of words did things to him. "I think we can do that."

"One of the men who attended those games is Wig Hardy."

"Wig?"

"Wiggins Hardy. Wig is a mechanic, and when he and Gus were in their thirties, they co-owned a shop together. According to what I could dig up, it didn't end well. He claimed Gus swindled him out of several thousand dollars."

"But he came to the poker games. Why would he do that if he was angry at Gus?" Beckett cracked his knuckles.

"Keeping enemies closer and all that. Or maybe if he'd been swindled he was hoping to make some money back. Detective Holmstead said the games probably weren't more than fifty bucks, but my source says sometimes it was as high as fifteen thousand dollars. That's a lot of cash."

"And motive for murder." They needed to talk to this Wig Hardy guy. Or do a little more snooping. "I may have a way to get into his financials without a warrant."

"Which won't hold up in a court of law if it incriminates him. The case will get tossed, Beckett. If he's responsible for my brother's conviction and for attacking me, he's not getting off the hook on inadmissible evidence in court." She tapped her fancy fountain pen on her sleek desktop.

Once again, she was proving they worked from opposite sides of the law. Beckett would snoop, then find another way to gain that hard evidence to convict. "Then what do we do, Counselor?"

"Well, it's not against the law to hire surveillance as long as no bugs are used. And I happen to know a guy who has a PI license in about twenty-five states, including Mississippi and Tennessee. He also happens to be sitting in my waiting area… doing surveillance on *me*."

Beckett chased her trail of thinking. Good idea. He rose from the chair and ambled to the door. "Looks like you and Wilder have been having a nice get-to-know-you tête-à-tête yourselves." He poked his head into the hall and hollered for Wilder. When he appeared, he asked, "How long did you say you were going to be in town?"

Wilder groaned. "I know that face. What do you want?"

EIGHT

It was Friday afternoon, and Aurora might go stir-crazy. The weather had cleared up to sunny and in the high fifties. Felt warmer though. The last two days had been nothing but rain. She was sick of rain and clouds and gloom.

Aurora stewed and paced her room like a caged animal, running down the events from the last few days. Wilder had been following Wig Hardy since Tuesday night when they'd decided to put surveillance on him. Most of the court cases had been pushed back; she'd only had to be in court twice. It was the nights that were extremely difficult, after Beckett retired to his room when she was left alone with thoughts of Kelly—seeing her family grieve by the casket. Aurora would make sure her killer was arrested and convicted, but that might not erase her own guilt.

Her freedom had been stolen. She had been driven from her home and was stuck here. While the inn was beautiful and comfortable, she wanted her life back. Aurora needed some space. Fresh air. Fresh hope. "Counselor?" Beckett knocked on the adjoining room door.

"Come in."

Beckett entered.

"Any news? Wilder come up with anything on Wig?"

"Not so far. He says the guy is boring other than his daily trips to the casinos in Tunica."

Which proved he was a gambler, and losing money could motivate someone to murder. That's when Aurora became aware Beckett wasn't in sheriff's clothing. He wore faded jeans, frayed around the ankles, cowboy boots with squared toes and a flannel shirt with a white T-shirt underneath. It was topped by a heavy denim jacket lined with wool and brown corduroy collar and cuffs. He did casual extremely well. Her pulse spiked.

"What are you about to do?" She gestured to his attire.

"What we're about to do. Throw on some jeans. You do own jeans, right?" A lopsided grin slid across his face.

"Yes. Where are we going?"

"You need a break. So we're getting out for a while and going to your dinner buddy's place."

She frowned. "Mitch Rydell is not my— You know what, forget it. Why are we going to

Mitch's?" His very name seemed to ruffle Beckett's feathers.

"Horseback riding. Fresh air. Countryside. Knock when you're ready."

"Does he know we're coming?"

"I made sure to call." A challenge of some sort flickered in his eyes. She wasn't going to get into Mitch Rydell again. It wasn't worth it, so she let it drop.

"Fine with me, but I don't have jeans here. I need to go home."

"Fine." Beckett grabbed his keys and drove her home to change. In thirty minutes, they were at Mitch's stable and saddling the sweetest Appaloosa horses on the planet.

"I should tell you, I haven't been on a horse since I was a teenager." Aurora climbed on and grabbed the reins, noticing Beckett watching her a little too closely.

"Well," he said, and cleared his throat, "you look like you remember pretty well." He mounted his horse like a guy from a cologne commercial, then kissed the air twice and nudged his horse on the sides with his foot. Aurora nudged her horse, too, and they set out across Mitch's pasture.

"So, where are we going?" Aurora asked as the horses went at an easy pace.

"Where do you want to go?" Beckett asked softly. "We can go wherever you want."

Was that a bit of subtext?

"I'd like to go to the beach. Can we ride to one?" she teased.

"You're a fan of warm weather?"

"Yes. Definitely. I could live in Florida or Cancun." She laughed as they moseyed across pure pastureland. Cows grazing. Enormous hay bales dotting the hills, the air crisp but not uncomfortable. The smell of spring ebbing and flowing, but the fear of someone watching never far from the back of her mind. She scoped out their surroundings just in case. "Are you sure we should be out here in the open like this?"

"You'll be fine."

He tucked his hand inside his coat pocket and retrieved a pair of dark sunglasses. Talk about being the front-runner for a cowboy magazine cover model. Aurora fought the urge to drool like a moron.

"I thought we might ride out by Hope Lake. They have some great trails. Lots of nature. You a fan of nature?"

"I like the outdoors, but I won't turn down a weekend at the spa." She could use a massage, with all her coiled muscles, but this ride was definitely helping. So was the company. "This was exactly what I needed, Beckett. Thank you."

"You're welcome."

The jittery feelings wore away as they settled into a nice pace and rode to the lake.

"So you like the beach. You have a beach house, Miss High-Cotton?" he teased.

She snickered. "No, but I've considered it. Maui. The Virgin Islands. I don't care where."

"I've thought about maybe hitting the beach sometime in the near future. Not as fun alone, though." He turned his head, but she couldn't see his eyes behind the sunglasses. Couldn't read him. Was he implying he'd like to visit the beach with *her*?

"No, they're not." Was she implying she'd go with him? This was ridiculous.

They rode quietly. He seemed to be struggling with something. Couldn't be the beach trip. She wasn't going on vacation with a man who wasn't her husband, and Beckett wasn't that kind of guy anyway.

They made their way to Hope Lake, where the water glistened under the sunshine. A few people were out taking strolls, walking dogs and having a good time.

"So…I was thinking about Wilder's offer the last couple of days. Since you're my attorney for all intents and purposes, you can't divulge any of this." He slowed, then stopped. Aurora reined her horse in, too.

She knew it. Knew he'd pondered it more than

he'd let on, and with Wilder in town, it had been weighing on him. "Have you reconsidered the offer?"

"Maybe. They help so many people. They go all over the world…even warm places."

Warm places. Sounded divine.

"What do you think, Aurora? Should I go?" He wrapped the leather reins around his fingers, let them out and wrapped them again.

He was asking her counsel? Her first instinct was to tell him no. To stay right here in Hope. The people needed him. He was honest and full of integrity, which was what a town needed in a sheriff, a leader. He was more than qualified. But she was being selfish. Keeping him here was like keeping her stuck in the inn. Caged. He needed to fly. To travel the world and put all of his experience and expertise to good use. Not to mention it might be too difficult seeing him every day and only in a sheriff's capacity. Because no matter what she felt, their line of work and living in a small town was going to be the driving wedge between them.

"When would you have to go?" she asked, trying to keep her voice from cracking. Her world without Beckett Marsh in it seemed bleak. Like the cloudy, rain-filled days she'd just experienced.

"I'm talking hypothetically. But if I do take the job, I certainly wouldn't go until you're safe.

Until we find who really killed Gus McGregor and who's been attacking you. And I'd have to put some things in order personally, and professionally." He licked his bottom lip. "But what do you think? Should I do it? Should I leave Hope?"

To tell him not to go wouldn't be right. Even if it was what she wanted. She couldn't hold him back like she suspected his mother might be doing indirectly, either. Mrs. Marsh had been clear the day they'd had muffins that she enjoyed her son nearby and safer. Not to mention Beckett had kept Aurora from divulging the truth about where she was staying, thus protecting his mother.

"Beckett, I think you are talented and skilled. No one is braver. No one is stronger. Smarter. You have all these amazing abilities and experience that you could be using all over the world. People need you. But you have to make that decision on your own."

He leaned across his horse and searched her eyes. "What people, Aurora? Who needs me?"

Aurora fell into his gaze, her mouth turning dry, the feel of his soft fingertips on her chin turning her to a puddle. *She* needed him.

"Aurora, I should tell you something. I've been...I don't know how...but—" He inched toward her.

Her breath hitched.

Beckett Marsh was going to...to kiss her.

And she wanted him to.

Anticipation mingled with his woodsy scent and descended upon her as he continued his slow-moving mission to her lips, his gaze locked on hers, waiting for her protest at any moment.

He wouldn't get one from her.

Aurora's stomach dipped and a fever sprang in her chest.

She closed her eyes as Beckett's nose grazed hers.

Crack!

The horses whinnied and Aurora's rose up on its hind legs, then shot forward, nearly knocking her from the saddle. She screeched, panic replacing that sweet, warm rush.

Another gunshot echoed through the woods.

Bark splintered from the tree she darted past. "Beckett!" she hollered, and tugged on the reins, but her horse continued to speed through the trees.

Beckett held tight as his horse reared, spooked from the gunfire. Aurora was already up ahead, her horse wildly running as she fought to get it in line, to no avail. The horse charged for the ravine.

Sweat beaded around his upper lip and temples as he pitched forward and kicked the horse's sides to move even faster. "Yah! Yah!" he boomed as he rode against the wind, moisture blowing from his eyes. He'd been riding since he was a kid. Aurora hadn't been on a horse in ages, and he feared the horse might buck her.

Another shot rang out. Where were they coming from? Sniper? Skilled gunman?

If he hadn't been terrified of Aurora getting bucked off, going over the side of the ravine or getting tossed and breaking her neck, he would have followed the sounds to try to track the shooter. He had experience.

Up ahead, Aurora pleaded with her horse, but another shot fired and bark exploded over her head.

Someone must be on higher ground, keeping himself concealed. He'd have to be on horseback, too, in order to keep up with how fast Beckett and Aurora were moving. But who?

Beckett continued to race after her, gaining speed. He kept his head ducked as he galloped under bare tree branches. The edge of the ravine was now only a few feet ahead.

"Beckett!" she called again.

"Hang on, Aurora! Yah!" he hollered again until he finally made it to her side. "Grab the saddle horn and hang on." No time to pull her onto his horse. He'd have to slow it this way. She obeyed his order and he snatched the reins on her horse with his left hand, keeping a grip on his own reins with the other. "Whoa!" He drew back with all he had, pulling the bit farther into the horse's mouth.

One more powerful tug and the horse slowed and then halted.

Beckett scanned the tree line.

Aurora's face had paled, her eyes wide, hands shaking. He grabbed them and held tight. "Let's get out of here. I don't know where the shooter is." Seemed like he'd been squeezing off rounds strategically, leading Aurora straight for the ravine.

Beckett had promised her she was safe. He'd brought her out here to spend time with her, to test out her feelings, and he'd almost gotten her killed. He was off his game. She was messing with his head, his heart.

Beckett led them under a dense covering of forest, keeping a hand on Aurora's reins. Her hair had fallen from the signature knot she kept on the back of her neck. "Aurora, words can't tell you how sorry I am. I promised you everything would be okay, and I failed," he choked.

"Beckett Marsh! What are you talking about? Bringing me out here was exactly what I needed. You sensed that. And I could have gone over the ravine, but I didn't. Because you were here. You did protect me."

Is that what she called protection?

"Still, I'm sorry."

"Well, don't be."

When she kept silent, he turned toward her. The sweetness on her face. It was all he could do not to drag her off the horse and into his arms and go for that kiss again. He wasn't sorry for attempting it, but it would have been a mistake in the end. And if he hadn't been so swept up in her, he might have noticed someone watching. Aurora thought he was brave. Capable. He'd needed to hear that. It was what had sent him spiraling over into that kiss. A kiss she might have welcomed. The moment was over now.

He had to stay laser sharp. Keep his eyes and ears open.

"Are you thinking this could have been Trevor Russell?" Aurora asked, finally sounding more like her confident self.

Good. Back to business. Back to the investigation. "Yes. I'm also wondering if more is going on here. Every shot was right above your head or near you. Like whoever did it didn't want to take you out with a bullet, but cause you to go over that ravine."

Aurora instinctively touched her throat. "But why?"

Beckett had been mulling that over. "The clothes being shredded. The note and bloodstained gavel. It's a game of cat and mouse."

Aurora's lip quivered. "Why would someone play dangerous games with me? And what's the end game?"

Beckett didn't want to voice the end game.

"Trevor Russell isn't sadistic. He wouldn't toy with you like this. When I went after Parker Hill, I wanted him dead. I wanted revenge. Vengeance— it wasn't a game."

She searched his eyes, as if begging for him to continue. He didn't owe her the truth, but if something did develop between them, she'd deserve it. Might as well put it out there and see where it landed. "I've been fixating on what you said about me being the judge and jury—"

"I had no right to say that, Beckett."

"But you were right and called me on it. Made me think." Beckett had needed that kind of honesty, regardless of the fact she'd said it in the heat of the moment. People rarely put up a fight or told him the hard things. They were too intimidated, and Beckett didn't mind because he rarely wanted to hear difficult truths. But not Aurora. She never backed down. "Sometimes, I think I am exactly that."

When God had seemingly failed Beckett with Meghan, and he'd seen an immense amount of needless bloodshed and tragedy, somewhere along the way, Beckett had assumed God's role, as if he knew better than the Almighty. It'd taken Aurora chewing him up and spitting him out to see it.

Aurora's hands had stopped shaking, but she didn't offer to take the reins back. Maybe, like Beckett, she was enjoying the closeness between them. "What do you mean you wanted revenge? What did you do?"

Truth time. Ashamed to admit it but needing to confide in her he pushed back the nerves and carried Aurora back with him. To another time. Another Beckett.

"Parker Hill is the man who was obsessed with Meghan. When he found out we were engaged, things escalated, but like I said before, he was the mayor's son and he skirted the law. Once we were married, we had planned to move here, and I hoped that would be the end of him. Now, in hindsight, I think he'd have followed us anywhere."

Aurora shifted in the saddle but remained quiet.

"I was offered a position with the Secret Service." Turning down Washington had been hard. The thought had been exhilarating.

"Wow, Beckett. Why didn't you take it?"

"I wanted to be closer to Mama. Be in a less dangerous job, give her some peace. Meghan accepted that and was fond of small towns—just ready to be out of hers after all that had transpired."

Aurora rubbed her lips together. "I see."

She was holding back. "You never clamp down on your opinions. Don't start now, Counselor."

She opened her mouth. Closed it. "You've been trying to shield your mother from my situation. I respect you want to give her less anxiety and your current station allows for that…but I wonder…are you happy? Are you doing exactly what *you* want?"

Was he? For the most part. "Yeah."

"Then why the hypothetical question earlier? If you're content, then moving and accepting another offer would be a moot point. Seems to me, part of you longs to accept." This right here was why she was the best attorney he'd ever met. She didn't skim surfaces—she dug deep. But he wouldn't admit the earlier conversation had been more about him digging for answers to how she felt about him than anything else. He might never know thanks to the shooter. "You're right. I was just talking. Let's drop it." He needed to pay attention to their surroundings better.

Her horse balked, ears twitching. Aurora's sight darted around the woods.

Beckett studied the perimeter, listened. "He's not spooked. You can relax." He'd worry for them both.

They ducked under a low-hanging branch. Only about a mile now from Mitch Rydell's ranch, out of the secluded woods. He never should have led her away from the public, but he'd wanted to be alone with her.

"Beckett?" Aurora asked delicately. "We got sidetracked and you never finished telling me what happened to Parker Hill."

He'd been ready to divulge this several minutes ago. Now he wanted to hit the dusty trail. Would Aurora still call him brave, strong, skilled when she learned how far he'd fallen? He bit back the shame, gathered as much courage as he could muster and said a quick prayer that she wouldn't think less of him.

"If you don't feel comfortable, Beckett, I understand."

He'd paused too long.

"It's not that, Aurora. I want to tell you. I'm not…proud of myself."

"You can trust me with your past." The gentleness in her voice gave him a nudge.

"When I thought he wasn't going to get justice, I went into a blind rage. I became everything he was. Stalked him. Stayed outside the law to do it. And one night I approached him. He said some things about Meghan I didn't like and the next thing I knew my hands were wrapped around his throat with no intention of releasing until he was dead." He quaked from the memory. "Wilder suspected I'd gone off the edge. He followed me. Saved me from going too far. And he'd found the evidence needed to put Parker away for good. If I'd listened to him, helped him, I wouldn't have almost murdered Parker and lost several months of my life in an obsessed blur."

She stared at her hands, the silence undid him, but he didn't dare say a word.

His chest tightened, leaving him short of breath. He had to know what she was thinking. He couldn't bear it if she thought of him differently, but she deserved the truth and it had felt right telling her.

Finally, her eyes met his. No contempt. No judgment. Not even a wrinkle of disappointment. But then Aurora was the least judgmental person he'd ever known. She was kind and considerate of everyone, even if she appeared standoffish upon a first impression. The glass was always half full, and that's what made her excellent at her job.

Unlike Beckett.

Who saw everyone with some kind of automatic stain on their record.

"Beckett, you're a good man. You can't let that one grievous act scar you. You can't."

His pounding chest stilled. This woman was making him feel secure. Safe.

"I know," he murmured.

"Thank you for trusting me, Beckett."

"Now you know why I think Trevor is still on the list and Oliver, too, but what about other enemies? Could it be Franco Renzetti?"

Aurora slipped her bottom lip between her teeth. "He murdered Oliver's son. He never came after me. Even after Severin died in prison, he never came. Why would he now? And toying with a person isn't Franco's MO. He'd just blow me up. Like he did Hayden Benard."

They crossed the pasture toward Mitch's stables. "Well, so much for getting out for a little living."

"I think we've discovered there's not going to be any life until we stop whoever's after me." Aurora's lips turned south.

"In case it is Franco, I'm going to give Wilder a call and have one of his guys nose around and see what ol' Franco has been up to in Chicago." Beckett released his hand on Aurora's reins as they reached the stable. "Why Chicago? You hate the cold."

Aurora ran her fingers through the horse's mane. "After Richie died, I didn't feel like I had a purpose anymore. I mean the whole point of going into law was to free him. So when I was offered the opportunity, it came with a huge perk. I could take on pro bono cases. As many as I could maintain, along with the billable hours at the firm. If I couldn't help Richie, I could help others who couldn't afford decent counsel. For three years I did that and carried all my other cases, too, several of them big and newsworthy. Severin wasn't my first major client."

"Papers say you and he…"

"We weren't. Romantically involved. I admit he was charming and I believed him when he said he wasn't involved in extortion. He said all the right things. His finances checked out. Everything was circumstantial. I thought he was branded a mobster because of his father, and I could relate. Being labeled a low-class nobody because my family was. He preyed on that."

"I'm sorry."

"Not as sorry as I am. I messed up cross-examining the detective, and I hate that. The cardinal rule is never ask a question you don't know the answer to. I had no idea the detective had personal knowledge of Severin shaking down a store owner for protection money fifteen years prior when he'd been a patrol officer."

"He was never charged?"

"Nope. So no record. But that testimony is what swayed the jury and put Severin away. Turns out he did deserve prison. Can't say he deserved what happened to him on the inside."

"The hit? I believe I read that somewhere." Beckett dismounted and helped Aurora, and they passed off their horses to one of Mitch's stable hands.

"Yes. Rival crime family."

All the more reason to have Wilder's team look into Franco Renzetti.

Aurora waved at Mitch Rydell. The two-dinners guy. Beckett needed to shove down the jealousy. Mitch was a nice guy. They made small talk a few minutes, Mitch never lingering too long on Aurora or flirting. Good. Beckett would hate to have to snuff him out.

They rode back to the inn, conversation at a minimum and the tension a little higher. He hadn't brought up the almost-kiss and neither had Aurora, but he'd been thinking about it. Had she?

He locked the doors to the Tahoe and they entered the lobby. A man with salt-and-pepper hair and a suit that probably cost more than Beckett's yearly salary stood by the desk. He made his way forward. "Aurora."

Beckett blocked his path to Aurora. If he wanted her, he'd have to plow through Beckett first. The expensive suit and cologne and demeanor—this guy could be on Franco Renzetti's payroll.

"And you are?"

"Oliver Benard."

NINE

Aurora's throat clogged. Beckett stood like a strong tower in front of her. She appreciated his attempt to protect her, but he couldn't be her constant shield.

A verse came to mind about God being her strong tower and refuge in times of trouble. She hadn't had a decent track record of running to Him in those times.

"I've been trying to call you for weeks, Aurora." Oliver peered around Beckett, and Aurora scooted to the side. Beckett cast his arm out as a barrier.

"Beckett," she said, and laid her hand on his rock-solid arm. If Oliver meant to harm her, he wouldn't do it in front of witnesses or in front of Beckett—unless he had a death wish.

Beckett lowered his arm and made a minimal move aside.

"What are you doing here, Oliver?" Aurora asked. Beckett gave him the glower only Beckett could, and Oliver broke eye contact. "How long have you been in town?" Beckett asked. "Since your meeting with Kelly Marks? You may have been one of the last people to see her alive."

Oliver might defend scary men, but he'd never been up against Beckett. A swell of pride took residence inside her chest.

"I came into town for that meeting, and I left right after. But I got word she died, and I'm back." He turned to Aurora. "Kelly was my last resort when you wouldn't answer or return my calls, Aurora."

"So why not show up like now? Why go to the judge?" Beckett demanded.

Rather excellent line of questioning, too.

"Because I needed to know Aurora's mental state."

"My mental state?" Aurora stepped in front of Beckett. "Oliver, what is going on? Your messages said we needed to talk. They were vague at best, and there was no mention of how I was holding up mentally."

"Could we talk privately?" He stole a peek at Beckett.

"Not gonna happen, pal." Beckett folded his arms across his chest.

Oliver huffed. "We can sit right over there at the café, and you, Mr. Whoever You Are, can sit right here and watch us the whole time."

"Beckett," Aurora insisted. "I'll be fine." She motioned Oliver toward the tables. "I'll be right there. Order some coffee or something if you like."

Oliver nodded and strode to a table in the corner.

Beckett leaned down and whispered, "Are you sure? You don't have to do anything you don't want to."

"Except when you tell me to."

His mouth twitched. "Well, when I tell you what to do, it's to keep you safe."

"Blah diddety, blah-blah-blah." She heaved a sigh.

Beckett chuckled. "And also, I know you haven't been interested in talking to him. If you're not ready…you're not ready. A man should wait for a woman until she is."

"I'll remember you said that." She'd also remember the tingles across her skin this very moment. While he was rough and demanding, Beckett could be quite the gentleman. "I'm ready to talk to him now. I…I want to hear him out. I think he's on the up-and-up, Beckett."

He touched her nose. "You're too good, Counselor. But don't change," he said with a muted tone. "Now, go on. I'll be right here."

"Sir, yes, sir." She saluted and turned, then spun back around. "You're too good, Sheriff.

Don't change." The way his eyes heated nearly melted her.

Oliver was drumming his thumbs on the table. It was uncomfortable seeing him. Running away, not attending the funeral. Being the sole cause of his sorrow… Shame popped in a flush across her cheeks. "I'm sorry for not coming to Hayden's funeral. I should have. I'm sorry for many things, Oliver—"

"Aurora, stop." He laid his hands flat on the table. "I understand why you left. I was angry about it at first. I expected…I don't know. Nothing you said or did could have changed what happened to my son."

"But I should have supported you. I didn't know what to do."

"You made a mistake, Aurora." His eyes locked on hers. She waited for flames of anger. Resentment. Judgment.

She found none.

"I know. I was afraid and I ran away from it all." And here she was, not escaping it. Oliver was in her face, forcing her to acknowledge those mistakes, and for what? "Why are you here? Why now?" She scooted her chair closer to the table and leaned in. "You know how this appears, Oliver, right? You are an attorney."

"I didn't kill Kelly Marks. Your friend over there is probably right. I may have been the last to see her alive. But I left town after we talked. I just read about her death, and I had no choice but to approach you in person. I'm aware of the Bledsoe boy's case and that you're in some trouble."

"Where did you read it?"

"Online."

"So you've been back in Chicago since your meeting?"

"No," he said warily. "I've been in Memphis. Visiting friends from college."

Convenient.

An internal whisper reminded her of his courtroom face. Stoic. Unyielding to any emotion yet controlled and almost friendly.

Same face.

Was this a courtroom proceeding to him?

"Why did you meet with Kelly? Why call her? And what does my mental state have to do with anything?"

Oliver checked to see where Beckett was. Eyeing them like a hawk a couple feet away. "I've been keeping up with you over the years. Watching."

Thoughts of Meghan's stalker slithered up her spine. "Clarify, please."

Oliver tented his hands. "Not like that. But I've changed since Hayden died. Losing someone you love does that."

"I know," she whispered.

"I've kept tabs on you. For fear Franco might come for you. I'm always sleeping with one eye open. When I heard about the Bledsoe boy, I thought maybe you were feeling guilty about Hayden and I don't want you to. When you wouldn't answer my calls, I turned to the only person I know you've trusted over the years. Judge Marks. I thought she could tell me how you were doing mentally. After all that happened. She might be able to soften you up to call me, to offer to see me of your own free will."

"She tried. I've been ashamed, Oliver." Afraid to face the music. She was afraid right now.

"I know," he said. "And she told me that the Bledsoe boy didn't remind you so much of Hayden as he did Richie. All those pro bono cases. I never understood why you attacked them with such gusto. Until losing Hayden and not getting any justice."

If Oliver didn't feel he'd received justice for Hayden—and he hadn't—then could he be sitting right here bald-faced lying to her? What would be the point? Why call Kelly? Why not show up like he was now?

"Did you tell Kelly not to share with me that you'd been in touch with her? Because she never told me once you'd phoned her. That's odd." She studied him, trying to crack through the blank face to see if she could find a single shred of malice.

"I didn't. I suppose she thought you might be upset and even more determined not to answer my calls if you assumed I'd been badgering her. Which I hadn't been. I just needed to know how you were and you wouldn't answer my calls to tell me."

Aurora tightened her lips.

"I know that face, Aurora. There's nothing malicious here. Hayden will have been gone two years February fifteenth. Feels like time to make amends. I don't have anything to do with the mess you're in. I think probing into Richie's conviction is stirring up a hornet's nest. Kelly told me you were back at it. Any leads?"

Discussing the investigation was out. While she struggled to believe Oliver was the one at the helm of these attacks, there was still a slight possibility. If she could only figure out what this conversation had to do with it. Unless he was creating an alibi that would require her to testify in court. To sit in that chair and tell the jury his son's death had been because of a slipup in court and he had come all this way to offer her grace and let her off the hook—well, they'd eat that up. See Oliver as the hero.

That was, if she lived through this. But even if she didn't and Oliver was charged, he'd have this lovely testimony and the sheriff as a witness because it was obvious Beckett could hear every word. The man wasn't going to let a possible suspect out of earshot. Beckett would have to testify that he had heard Oliver extend grace. And that would go far with a jury.

"Aurora? What is it?"

She slid her sight to Beckett, and he stood taller as if to come to her aid. She gave him an almost-invisible shake of her head to keep him at bay. "I made a mistake that cost your son his life. You should hate me."

Oliver laid his hand over Aurora's. "You couldn't have known Franco would retaliate that way. I didn't even know."

"He came after the one person you loved most when he should have come after me."

"And one day he'll pay for killing my son. But you shouldn't have to."

If Oliver was the real deal, Aurora didn't know how to respond. How could someone offer her grace? Someone innocent had paid her penalty. She didn't deserve it. "Oliver, I hope you mean this. I want to believe that you do. I need to believe it. And, if so, I don't know what to say but thank you. But I have to say, if you're not being forthright, Beckett Marsh will sniff it out and hunt you down. I hope you know that. And if you didn't, you do now."

Oliver's eyes widened a fraction. "Aurora, I understand it's hard to wrap your brain around.

But I am being honest, and I don't take umbrage with the fact you might believe I'm trying to kill you." His lips quirked. "In fact, I'd say you'd lost some spark if you didn't think that. It does appear ominous."

Or, at the very least, odd timing. And yet her heart ached because she did want grace and to be forgiven, but even she couldn't forgive herself. So why should anyone else?

Oliver stood. "If you need any help regarding your brother's case, you have my number. Call if you need me." He hugged her and Aurora spotted Beckett's jaw tense, but she didn't feel fearful. No, Oliver Benard may very well have changed for the better, though through tragic circumstances.

She walked Oliver to the door and watched him leave.

"So I'll hunt him down, will I?" Beckett met her and slung his arm around her.

She forced herself not to lean into him. "You know you will."

"You can take that to the bank. Whoever is responsible. I won't lie—he sounded sincere but—"

"You think he's the one terrorizing and attacking me."

"Oliver has motive. He'd know where to hit you to make you feel most vulnerable. The safety of your home—you had to leave Chicago and now your home here. Your suits. Kelly. I can't say what he does or doesn't know about cars, but he's a defense attorney. He knows dozens of shady characters willing to do some dirty work in return for a top-notch attorney."

Aurora struggled with what was true and what might be pretense. Could someone simply extend grace like that, or was it a ploy? "Why would he care that I'm inquiring into Richie's case?"

"He might not. But he could easily be using this as a prime opportunity. While we've been assuming Gus's killer is after you, maybe Oliver Benard wants you to think that." Beckett held Aurora's chin. "Can you tell me without a shadow of doubt that Oliver Benard is innocent?"

Without a shadow of a doubt? "No, I can't say that."

"I'm going to do some more digging on him." Beckett guided Aurora to the stairs. "And another question—how did Oliver Benard even know you were here?"

Aurora grabbed the railing, afraid she might be sick. Beckett had nearly taken a life. If a man as honorable as Beckett Marsh could stoop that low, then how much easier would it be for a man who didn't share all of Beckett's honorable qualities?

Not that Oliver was a bad man, but he wasn't in his line of work to help the less fortunate. He was in it for the money and always had been. He'd said he'd changed. Had he really?

"Are we changing rooms or locations again?" She was tired of hiding. Running.

"No. This is the safest place for us. Public. We're going to stand firm."

At least until someone knocked them down again.

Inside the room and unable to sleep, Aurora made a cup of tea and curled up on the couch. Beckett knocked on her door and she gave him permission to enter. Dressed in navy athletic pants and a Memphis Grizzlies T-shirt, he looked like a man about to shoot hoops, not investigate a murder. "You want tea?"

He snorted. "I'm gonna pass. What's going on in that terrifyingly brilliant mind?" He grabbed a light throw Aurora had brought from home and draped it across her lap, the gesture sending little rainbows dancing around her heart. "Other than you were cold."

"How do you know that?"

"When you break out the fuzzy slippers. Otherwise, you go barefoot, because you drop your shoes the minute you enter a room." He slunk onto the other end of the small sofa.

He'd figured all that out? "Now, I'm thinking I should make a list of everyone from Richfield to Hope who could be a suspect, including Trevor Russell and Oliver Benard."

He grasped her foot, then rubbed it. "Wilder

called. He said this Wig Hardy guy seems clean other than his gambling problem, and since you won't allow me to let him riffle through his financials and see if skeletons pop out from the vaults, I can't say whether that assumption is true or not. And I can't keep Wilder sitting on a man who may not have anything to do with Gus's murder. Maybe you should talk to Gus's widow about Wig."

Aurora sipped her jasmine tea, not as rich as Felicity's over at the Read It and Steep. "I can. But it seems to me that Gus kept Darla on a need-to-know basis."

"Or she doesn't want to further involve herself and she's playing dumb. What about her sister?"

"Linda? What about her?"

"She did the books at the mechanic shop, according to the files. Maybe she can help us out, tell us if Gus was doing underhanded business and who with. If he rooked Richie out of money for work on cars, he probably cheated everyone else on the planet, too, including other employees. I read over a few testimonies backing up Richie's claim, but that only solidified the DA's case against Richie."

"You've been doing some late-night studying."

"I haven't been able to sleep much, and I can hear better when I'm awake." He settled a throw pillow on his lap and yawned.

"You should sleep, Beckett. I know you're

trained to stay awake for days on end, but I feel bad." She also knew Beckett was right. "Can you hand me that notepad on the table beside you and the pen?" She needed to add to the list of people who might want her dead. "I say we go back to Richfield tomorrow and poke around a little more. Talk to some of the old employees that are still around and the people who might have been at those poker games, as well as Linda and Darla."

"I say we let Wilder do it. He has a way with getting people to talk. You're too emotionally connected. Remember your conversation with Dwight Holmstead? Lasted a hot minute before you went in for the kill."

She had treated the detective as a hostile witness. But she had a bond with Darla. "True, but I'd like to talk to Darla and her sister myself."

Would Beckett compromise?

"I'll agree to that. Wilder takes the suspects, you take witnesses." His phone rang. "Wilder. We were just talking about you."

Aurora listened as Beckett and Wilder had a conversation and then he hung up.

"Well?" Aurora asked.

"He's leaving Richfield for the night, but while he was tailing Wig, he also checked into Oliver. Legally. He's taken a leave of absence from the firm. He didn't make any arrangements through his secretary, which, according to her, he always does."

"How did he discover all this? And legally?"

"Again, he's gifted at getting people to talk." He leaned forward. "Has Oliver ever taken time off like this before?"

"No." Oliver rarely used vacation time. The longest was after Hayden died. "When's he set to come back?"

"No date to return. Yet."

Could Oliver have fallen off the edge and plotted all this? The date of Hayden's death was approaching. He never said what specific friends in Memphis he was visiting. The more Aurora thought about the possibility, the sicker she became.

Beckett hadn't taken Aurora's advice on sleep. Instead, he'd spent the night making calls to hunt down Trevor Russell. They needed to talk, but family and friends weren't being cooperative. Which meant they were angry or hiding something.

He knocked on Aurora's door at 8:45 a.m. She opened it, hair pulled back in her tight knot, but she wore dressy jeans and a velvety white sweater. "I have to make a run to Sufficient Grounds before we head out to talk to Darla and Linda. The espresso machine is on the fritz again."

"So you need to jiggle the wires, then?" Beckett chuckled and held her purse while she shrugged into a knee-length gray wool coat. Didn't matter what she wore—she wore it classy.

Aurora tromped down the stairs. "I'm so sick of that machine."

"Do that many people need a cappuccino this early?"

"It's almost nine—on a Saturday. Of course they do. Katelynn says talk is already dying down about the motion. It typically does."

Until it didn't.

The weather decided to rise into the high fifties once again, making it feel like spring. Overhead, the clouds had parted to reveal bright sunshine.

"I think I know where Trevor Russell is. When we get back from Richfield, I'm going to go check it out. He has a fishing buddy that owns a cabin about fifty miles south of here." Beckett helped Aurora inside the vehicle.

"I still can't believe he'd do all this. I've seen him at church. And he's a youth leader."

"Christians aren't immune to grief, pain, anger or feelings of revenge. Trust me. If we don't let God deal with those emotions—if we entertain them—we can end up in a very dark place. At the very least, bitter and cynical." Even King

David—a man after God's own heart—committed murder. "We can fall fast, Aurora."

"I kind of gave up on my faith after Richie." Aurora gave a half shrug, uncertainty on her face. "But I feel guilty for that, too."

She seemed to feel guilty about everything. Beckett related. "Join the club."

"But you go to church faithfully."

"And I sit there as confused and unsure as any man. I don't only believe in God. I *know* Him. I don't understand Him and that bothers me. Evil should be punished and good rewarded, but it never seems to work that way."

"I agree. But we can't give up hope, can we?"

He had. Until recently. Until Aurora had opened his eyes to start seeing some good again. "I suppose not."

They pulled around back and parked, then Beckett followed her through the rear entrance and into the kitchen. A few teenage girls he recognized hustled and bustled to make special coffees and menu items. The sounds of laughter wafted from the front; the smell of freshly brewed espresso and cinnamon made his mouth water.

Aurora shrugged out of her coat and moved the stainless-steel machine a hair forward. "Did you move this?" she asked Katelynn.

"No. I don't even try anymore." Katelynn gave the machine the death stare. Was she mentally threatening it to work? With that expression, he'd get straight into working order if he was a coffee machine.

Aurora squinted and stared at the espresso machine.

"What's the matter?" Beckett asked.

"I don't know." She squatted and peered behind the stainless-steel counter. "Have you used it yet this morning?"

"A few times, but then it locked up. Not like before." Katelynn jerked her head when someone hollered for her. "Guess I'll tell them to order regular coffee." She sped off, muttering how boring that would be.

"I hate this thing. Can you believe there isn't even a warranty on it?" Aurora said as she scooched further behind the counter and unplugged the machine.

"I say nothing beats a good cup of black coffee."

"You would. Can you hand me that pink tool kit over there? I need to open the back of the machine, jiggle the wires."

The pink tool kit. Nice. "Yes, because one needs to look girlie while doing—"

"If you say men's work, you die." She snickered as he opened the tool kit and removed a screwdriver.

"I was going to say *handiwork*."

"Sure you were." She held out her hand.

"I can do it."

"So can I."

He admired her tenacity. "Yes, ma'am." Gently, he laid the screwdriver in her palm, and she went to work loosening the screw.

"Huh."

"What?"

"Feels tighter than I normally turn it." She leaned into it and grunted as she worked to unloosen the screw. "Seriously."

Beckett slipped the tool from her hand. "You the only one who opens the machine and jiggles the wires?"

"Unfortunately."

The screws were definitely tight, but he undid them and handed Aurora the screwdriver. He lifted the backing off and was hit with a wave of panic. "Move! Right now. Go!"

Aurora froze, then glared. "What on earth is wrong with you? And don't order me! I'm not a McDonald's menu item."

He didn't have time for fluffy and sweet. "Counselor, you unplugged the espresso machine and activated a dead man's switch."

"A dead man's switch…a bomb!" Aurora's flushed face blanched and she shook her head vehemently. "I'm not leaving without you! Can you deactivate it?"

Pressure built in his chest. Inside the espresso machine was plenty of dead space, and someone had planted a brick of C-4 with a digital timer attached. Someone had to know the espresso machine messed up often and Aurora would come to fix it, unplugging it, which had been the catalyst.

"Aurora," he said as calmly as possible, fear riding a tidal wave through his bones. "I want you to calmly but quickly go into the dining area. Tell them there's a gas leak. Nothing to worry about, but the fire department is on their way and they need to evacuate. Then call the fire department."

He turned to make sure she registered his words. Like a deer in headlights. No one would believe her. "Aurora, send Katelynn. Tell her there's a gas leak." He repeated his lines. No point having a stampede out there with the words "bomb threat." Not until he could turn the timer and see how much time they had. If he could get them out calmly, that was the way to go. If not, he'd cross that bridge when he got there. "Now. Then get out. I mean it."

Aurora paused, then bolted for the cashier station.

Beckett prayed, hoping God would hear and save them all. Did he have time to deactivate it? He didn't even have any tools!

Aurora rushed back to his side. "I told Katelynn. What can I do, Beckett?"

He worked carefully to turn the bomb. The timer wasn't facing him. He had to know how much time they had.

Any second they could all be blown to bits.

"I told you what you can do," he snapped. "Get out of here. Now."

Aurora rushed into the café and returned once more. This wasn't the time to ignore him.

"I told you to go," he said with force. He wanted her out. Unharmed. And this instant.

"Beckett, people aren't leaving fast enough! My employees are still working."

He moved at a snail's pace, careful not to bump the bomb. To set it off.

The timer turned and he read the minutes and seconds.

Oh, God. Help us!

"How many people are left, Aurora?"

"Like twenty or so. They—"

"No time! Go!" He needed to get them out. All of them. There was enough C-4 to take out the whole building.

"What's happening?" Katelynn shrieked.

Aurora pushed Katelynn through the back door. Beckett flew to the front. Time to cross the bridge. "Ladies and gentlemen, ya'll got to go this second. We have a bomb threat."

That put them in gear and caused a major panic. Women hollered and grabbed their children.

Men ushered them out the front door like a herd of cattle.

Sirens blared in the distance.

Aurora came through the front door into the dining area, helping shove people outside.

"What are you doing back in here? Get out!"

"I'm not leaving without you, Beckett!" Aurora screamed, determination set in her eyes.

When the last person was out, Beckett worked on crowd control with the fire department. Police cruisers arrived. Where was Aurora? She had been right beside him two seconds ago.

Beckett checked his watch.

Sixty seconds left.

Police and firefighters evacuated the area.

Katelynn stood on the sidelines crying.

He fought his way over to her. "Where's Aurora?"

"Johnna was in the bathroom. She's eight weeks pregnant and—"

"Where is Aurora?" he boomed.

"She went back in for Johnna!"

Forty-three seconds.

No!

TEN

Aurora couldn't leave Johnna. Only eight weeks pregnant, she'd been locked up in the bathroom vomiting. She had no clue what was going on. Aurora ran in the back entrance for fear no one would let her inside the front, her feet nearly coming out from under her.

Her whole body shook; even her teeth chattered. She had no idea how much time she had, but if she didn't go back in for Johnna what kind of person did that make her?

"Johnna!" she called, adrenaline racing through her veins. "Johnna!" She banged on the employee restroom door but no answer. She opened it.

Empty.

Had she gone out the front when Aurora came in the back?

A noise sounded and she whipped to the right. Johnna exited the walk-in freezer. "What's going on? Sorry. I got hot after I got sick. I hope—"

"Aurora!" Beckett's voice bellowed and echoed off the walls from the café area.

"We have to go, Johnna. Bomb!"

Johnna's face turned white and she bolted out the back door, no questions asked.

Aurora raced through the kitchen, past the barista workstation to the dining area. "Beckett!"

Beckett rushed her, mad and wild fear in his eyes, but as they locked on hers they revealed it wasn't fear for him, but her. Before she had a chance to run or utter a word, he tackled her like a force of nature, knocking the breath out of her.

His body enveloped her like a secure glove. "Tuck your head and close your eyes!"

She tucked as an earth-pounding boom overpowered her own thoughts, the blast sending them through the air and forward, searing heat licking at her.

Ears ringing, she shrieked bloody murder.

Stings pricked her skin.

Dear God in heaven! They were going straight through her storefront window like a rocket into space. She couldn't be sure if it was from the blast or if Beckett had propelled them through to safety.

Sirens.

Shouts.

Screams.

Smoke.

Fire.

Everything felt like slow motion, but it happened so fast her head swam. Beckett flipped in the air onto his back and landed with a horrifying thud on the cracked sidewalk littered with shards of debris and glass.

Aurora's head snapped upon impact, and she rammed Beckett's chin with her nose, warmth suddenly flowing. She let out a cry as the blood dripped into her mouth, and she coughed and sputtered as dirt and smoke filled her lungs. Her eyes burned.

First responders rushed to their aid, asking questions and prying her away from Beckett.

He wasn't moving.

Beckett wasn't moving!

Move! "Beckett! Beckett!" she wailed.

A frenzy of people crowded and separated them, dragging her away.

Her ears rang, and sounds were muffled.

"We have him, ma'am. We need to get you medical attention."

Firefighters worked on dousing the blazes.

A throng of onlookers stood by, fright and shock on their faces. Some videoed with their cell phones.

"Bomb. There was a bomb," she said as they wrapped a black wool blanket around her and loaded her in the back of an ambulance. "I'm fine. I'm fine!" she hollered, and craned her neck for Beckett.

Beckett wasn't moving.

"Miss Daniels, you have several lacerations and abrasions that need medical attention, and not that I need to remind you, but you flew about six feet through a glass window. You're not fine. You're in shock." She registered the young man who frequented Sufficient Grounds speaking to her but couldn't recall his name.

"But where is Sheriff Marsh? Is he okay? I need to know he's okay!" He'd come back in for her. If he was hurt… If he was… She couldn't possibly bear the blood of one more person on her hands.

A Scripture long forgotten sprang to mind: "Give your burdens to the Lord, and He will take care of you."

Could she? How? How did she give her burdens to the Lord without taking them back? She'd tried before and failed. *Lord, I don't know what to do! I'm not deserving. I failed Richie. I failed Oliver and Hayden. I failed You! So many times.* Had she ever truly trusted God with her problems? The ones she couldn't fix on her own? The ones she might have fixed better had she asked Him to help?

Carrying around this guilt wasn't healthy. But every time she tried to let it go, every single mistake she'd ever made played on a repeated loop in her mind.

"Aurora!" Blair McKnight fought the crowd and pushed her way to Aurora's side. "You're in one piece. Thank You, God." Blair hugged her neck and scowled when first responders brushed her away.

"Beckett. Have you seen him? Is he gonna make it?"

Blair's eyes filled with tears.

No. He had to be all right.

"Spit it out, Blair. I can't take it."

Blair covered her mouth. "I don't know. I heard someone say something about a chopper flying him to the Med in Memphis. But I can't get close enough to see anything. Holt's leaving Memphis now. Coming home. But I'll ride with you to the hospital." She ignored the man who'd been talking to Aurora and climbed inside without any protest from the EMT.

At the hospital, they picked shards of glass from her skin, cleaned wounds and gave her three stitches on her hand. Beckett had taken the brunt and she'd yet to hear any word on him.

Blair stayed by her side, uttering quiet prayers and rubbing her back. "Aurora, whatever Beckett did, he did to protect you. Please don't beat yourself up. I know that face. I felt the same way when Holt put himself in danger for me."

Aurora blinked back tears. "It's hard not to beat myself up. I'm responsible."

"No, you're not. Whoever set that bomb is. And Beckett is a grown man who makes his own choices. He chose to go back in after you. He chose to get involved. And, if my suspicions are right, he's chosen to love you."

"Love is strong emotion." So was guilt. "I don't want to have this guilt-noose around my neck, but I don't know how to let go, to wiggle loose. Whatever I need to do to be free." She had no peace.

Blair settled next to her on the hospital bed. "Aurora, you of all people should understand what it means to advocate for someone, to stand before a jury and judge and plead a case, a cause, and fight to declare a defendant innocent—even if they're guilty of the crime."

Aurora stared at her stitches, wincing at the tenderness. Or maybe it was the tenderness in her heart. "What's your point?"

"Jesus stood as an advocate for you. While the mud was slung and you were accused before the judge of all your sins, guess what? Jesus stood right there and defended you. Knowing you were guilty, but dying so you could have a clean slate. Like you did with Austin Bledsoe. Wiping the slate clean for him in a sense so he could have a second chance and turn from his mistake."

Aurora had never pictured Jesus as an advocate, an attorney. But He had pleaded her cause. Defended her. Declared her innocent and set her free, but she was still trying to convict and sentence herself to punishment.

"Aurora?"

She focused on Blair.

"Accept God's grace. Tell yourself it's permissible to move forward without the guilt."

Maybe it was time.

Blair's words from days earlier struck her core.

A man who's willing to sacrifice his life for you is more than worth admiring. He's worth loving.

Isn't that exactly what Jesus had done for her? Sacrificed His life out of love for her? Had she really given Him a chance? She'd spent most of the time pushing Him away because she didn't feel worthy enough to accept the amazing gift He'd offered.

Grace.

Forgiveness.

He'd paid a debt she should have.

Like Hayden had paid for a debt Aurora owed. Even if Oliver Benard was using forgiveness on a false pretense, she could still forgive herself and stop dragging a fatal mistake around with her every day. She had an advocate working on her behalf. Declaring her *innocent*. "But Richie deserves to have his name cleared."

"I'm not telling you to stop fighting or advocating for clients. I'm telling you it's time to live. To trust that God does love you and cares what happens to you. I'm telling you to take off the gloves and quit pounding yourself. Quit letting the enemy pummel you."

She'd told Beckett he thought he was God, acting as judge. But Aurora had been playing God a little bit, too. Carrying burdens she shouldn't. *Lord, forgive me. Help me to forgive myself and lift the guilt off me. Help me to surrender it all to You. And help Beckett.*

A sense of peace settled over her and she dared to think she felt a degree lighter just from confessing she'd been carrying problems and anguish she was never intended to carry.

"Where is she?"

Aurora snapped up her head. Beckett!

She jumped off the hospital bed and flinched, then there he was standing in her doorway, head bandaged and looking the worse for wear but not in the Med.

"You're alive!" She ran to him and threw herself against him. He gave a small grunt but wrapped his arms around her.

"Of course I'm alive."

"But I heard you were being medevaced to the Med."

"I don't have time for all that." His voice quieted. "I had to see about you."

Aurora touched his bandage. "Your head."

"Hard as a rock. Bumps and bruises, maybe a stitch or two, but I'm in working order. How about you?" He held her hand in his. "I hate this."

"I'm functional." She sighed relief. *Thank You, God. Thank You.* She suspected Beckett was giving her the fluffy version of his health, but he was standing there. And talking. Walking. She'd take it. "Was anyone else hurt?"

"Some minor injuries, but we got everyone out in time. Thanks to God for that. However, you can kiss your café goodbye. And, on either side of you, the florist shop and the eye doctor's office." Beckett finally seemed to notice Blair, who'd remained quiet by the bed. "Holt called while I was getting fixed up. He's on his way home."

"I know. So, on that note, I'll leave you two to talk." She left Aurora alone with Beckett.

She'd been so worried. Terrified. Her whole life had flashed before her, and the thought of Beckett not having a place in it had undone her.

But the only place available in her life was as a friend. Whether he stayed in Hope and certainly if he moved states away.

And she was still a defense attorney. Now, more than ever, she knew that people needed her to advocate on their behalf. She couldn't stop defending people. Couldn't stop being a lawyer.

Beckett would never stop being on the opposite side of the law, either. Even in Atlanta, he'd be working to put away the very people Aurora felt called to defend.

"You don't know how relieved I am to see you. You scared me half to death lying so still on the pavement."

"I was afraid I might have broken you." He toyed with her hair that had come loose and trailed his finger down her arm. "Forgive me for the brute force."

"Brute force saved my life." Her ribs would remind her of that for weeks to come. "Are you thinking what I'm thinking?"

Longing filled his eyes. "I doubt it."

She couldn't afford longing. In the end, they'd both get hurt. Common sense told her that. "Bomb. This could be Franco Renzetti. He used a bomb to kill Oliver's son."

"I know. But anyone can find out how to make one on YouTube. So we still can't rule out Trevor Russell."

"Or Oliver himself. He'd know exactly the kind of bomb Renzetti's guy used to take out Hayden and so many others. They all have a signature calling card." Aurora wasn't sure what Renzetti's man's style was. But if it matched exactly, then either Franco was behind this…or Oliver was. Trevor Russell wouldn't have the ability to discover that kind of detailed information. Neither would Gus McGregor's killer. Not that she could imagine anyway.

"I'm going to call the SWAT bomb expert who dealt with Hayden Benard's car bomb. See what matches and what doesn't. And I'm going to ride out to that campground and see if I can't find Trevor."

Aurora tucked a strand of hair behind her ear. "Beckett, whoever set this bomb couldn't be sure I'd be in the building. In fact, I speculate he didn't know at all. Who would be willing to blow up a building full of people to hurt me emotionally?"

"Not true. Someone picked the espresso machine. Could be random. Or they knew the barista would call you to fix it. Then you'd unplug it and boom! We can't be sure what the bomber did or didn't know." Beckett squeezed her uninjured hand. "As far as people willing to blow up folks to get to you… Unfortunately, Counselor, there are too many. Which is why you and me, we're like magnets from here on out."

How long until someone with enough force ripped them apart?

In one breath Beckett was telling Aurora they were stuck together. In the next, he was bringing Wilder back from Richfield to keep watch over her while he drove out to see if Trevor had hunkered down at his buddy's cabin. He could have put one of his deputies on Aurora-watch. They'd found zero evidence that any of his people had been behind this or leaked information; he'd grilled them intensely. But she still didn't trust them like she trusted Beckett.

Truth be told, Wilder had the skill set most of his deputies didn't have. If anyone could give him some peace because Beckett couldn't protect her, it was Wilder. But he had to go back to Atlanta on Monday and he couldn't send any of the other team members since they were all tied up on cases. His snooping around and talking to the few employees who had remained in Richfield had been a bust so far.

Beckett's entire body would be sore for weeks and his ears ringing for days. He suspected Aurora would be in the same boat. The glass had cut through his thick coat. Had he not been wearing it, the damage would have been much more severe. He'd never been more frightened than the moment he realized Aurora had gone back inside. The woman was brave, and he couldn't fault her for wanting to take care of her own and refusing to leave a team member behind. He'd have done the same thing.

But it was clear the minute he checked his watch and saw thirty seconds, the minute it dawned that they weren't going to make it out on their two feet: he cared about Aurora way more than he should.

She challenged him. Fought him at every turn. Forced him to change for the better.

Meghan, coming from a military family, had never batted an eye at what Aurora called Beckett's commands. He liked the way Aurora dished it out and stood up to him, even though he wasn't intentionally being a dictator.

He liked the way she fought for what she believed in, though he still wasn't sure she was fighting for the right people. But then, Beckett had to think about Richie. Each day, he'd realized even more that Aurora was right. Richie had gone to prison for a crime he hadn't committed. Sadly, it happened. And if Beckett wanted to be even more honest, he knew deep down Austin Bledsoe was a good kid who'd made the biggest mistake of his life. But that wasn't the case all the time. In fact, most times those kids went to juvie only to be let out to make the same mistakes repeatedly, and even bigger ones.

But was it right to punish everyone for the ones who truly deserved it?

No.

And someone needed to champion them.

He just wished it wasn't Aurora.

Trevor's blue pickup truck was parked next to a two-story cabin settled among a backdrop of woods. No smoke pluming from the chimney. Sometimes Beckett's job stank. He surveyed his surroundings as he climbed the steps to the front porch.

He listened a moment. No sound.

He knocked.

Knocked again.

Movement flashed through the window. What sounded like a scuffle inside had Beckett putting his sore shoulder to the door and ramming it open.

Trevor Russell lay in the middle of the living room floor, two chairs knocked over near him. He moaned and struggled to sit up.

Beer cans and bourbon bottles littered tables. The placed smelled like it needed airing out.

"Trevor," Beckett muttered. The man was a mess. Beckett helped him up, ignoring the rancid smell emanating from him. Whoo. Days on a binger here. Beckett eased him onto the couch. The guy was a soggy mess.

"Beckett," he slurred. "What are you doing here? You seen Bethany?"

Beckett's heart splintered a crack. He knew that grief well. The liquor had dulled Trevor's senses and let him see the past in a way that would only cause pain when he sobered. When Trevor pulled it together, he wouldn't be proud of this behavior. He'd repent and wish he hadn't succumbed to the very thing that ultimately killed his wife.

Drunkenness.

"I'm gonna make some coffee, man." If there was any coffee to be found.

"He killed my wife, Sheriff. She's gone and no one is going to remember. But I will. I'll remember." He slumped on the couch in a state of tears and a runny nose.

"I know he did." Beckett searched cabinets until he found instant coffee. Gross. It'd have to do, though. He made a cup and carried it back to Trevor. "Drink it. Now." He sat in a rickety chair by the couch as Trevor sipped the bitter brew.

By the count of the bottles and Trevor's state, he'd been in this cabin and nowhere else. Not able to have set a bomb or shred clothes. Make calls. No, the recent attacks on Aurora weren't Trevor's doing. But… "You throw that bottle into Aurora's house? Key her car? Make threats against her?"

Trevor wiped his nose.

Might not be fair to ask him this question when he was drunk. Wouldn't hold up in court. But he wasn't going to put him in the slammer for it, anyway. Aurora wouldn't press charges. By now he knew her well enough to make that call. And if she'd seen Trevor in this state, she'd only feel wretched.

"Nope." His eyes shifted, and he rubbed his hand on his jeans. Nervous gesture. He was lying or…

"What about Quent? He's not going to get

hauled in. But some serious stuff is going down and I need to rule out a few things." Aurora had too many possible enemies, and Beckett needed to scratch some of them off the list.

Trevor hiccupped. "He lost his mom. He lost it all."

"So he got mad and keyed her car. Did he also throw that bottle?"

Trevor finished the coffee and set his cup on the table with a clank. "He's just a boy."

"I know, man. I know. I'm sorry it all happened. But this, Trevor. This is not the way to deal with the grief. It only numbs it and makes it worse. This isn't who you are."

Trevor covered his face with his hands. "I don't know who I am without her!"

Beckett's chest tightened. "You're a man. A father. A firefighter. A friend. A child of God, and this is no way to behave as one. You know you'll feel guilty about it later."

"I feel guilty now." Trevor let loose a stream of sobs and Beckett sat beside him on the couch. He'd learned long ago that crying didn't make you weak. Crying helped heal. So he sat there while Trevor began the healing process and, in between sobs, told slurred stories of Bethany while Beckett silently prayed God would do what He did best and comfort Trevor Russell.

An hour later, Trevor admitted Quent had keyed

Aurora's car and thrown the bottle of Old Crow through her window. As far as phone calls and attacks, he didn't believe any of that had been Quent and neither did Beckett.

Trevor wasn't a killer. He was a broken man who needed to be fixed by God. Beckett shared most of his story with Trevor, leaving out almost murdering Parker Hill but including how isolation had been detrimental to his mental health. Trevor needed to stop isolating himself. Beckett had done that after Meghan and it only fed his bitterness and thoughts of revenge. Beckett cleaned Trevor up best he could until he could get him home. He led him to the Tahoe and drove him back to his house.

"Thanks for not judging me," Trevor said as Beckett led him inside.

"I'm learning I'm not a judge these days."

"I had no idea you'd been engaged." Trevor dropped his bag by the couch.

It had felt satisfying to be able to share his dark moment to help shed light on Trevor's. What happened to Meghan had been tragic, but right now it seemed like maybe God was using it for some good. To help Trevor Russell.

Beckett called their pastor while Trevor got cleaned up. Someone needed to be here with him to give him wise spiritual guidance. Quent was still staying with Trevor's parents. Beckett had suspects to cross off lists and, quite frankly, he'd missed Aurora. When Pastor Bradley arrived, Beckett left for the inn. Wilder opened the door to Aurora's room.

"Well?" she asked.

"Trevor's not our guy." He quickly briefed them.

Aurora scratched her head. "My mom called. She said she found some old boxes of Richie's in the storage shed. Asked if I wanted to go through them. I do."

"Then let's get some rest after the day we've had and tomorrow we'll head to Richfield. We still need to talk to Darla and her sister, Linda, about those books and business accounts."

"I'll be in my room if you need anything." Wilder shut the door behind him.

"Hi," Beckett murmured, as if he'd stumbled upon and seen Aurora for the first time.

"Hi."

Now what? "How's your hand?" He closed the distance between them, lifted her hand for gentle inspection, and to simply be close to her.

"Tender. Raw."

Like his heart. No amount of stitches would fix it.

He gazed into her eyes, wanting nothing more than to dip low and kiss her. Instead, he sighed. "We have a big day tomorrow. Go to sleep."

She didn't even bother to remind him he'd ordered her to bed. Aurora broke from his personal space and nodded as she turned. "Right. Long day. Smart idea."

Beckett hesitated at the door.

He wasn't making a mistake, was he? No. He couldn't let the way he felt get the best of him. Allowing himself to get emotionally tangled could be dangerous. But it was too late. He was already in over his head. He had to keep focused on the task. Acting on his feelings for Aurora would be too risky for a million different reasons.

He gave her one long glance, fighting the urge to draw her into his arms, and closed the door with a quiet click.

ELEVEN

Knocking on the adjoining room door woke Aurora. Her head pounded and she was sore and stiff. She crawled out of bed and slipped on her robe. "Come in," she rasped.

"Breakfast." Beckett bounded into the room as if he hadn't been blown out a window and shredded by glass. As if he hadn't knocked his head on the concrete. He'd even removed the bandage. A nasty abrasion near his temple remained as proof he had been almost killed. "Eat. We have to leave in an hour."

An hour? She glanced at the clock. It was almost noon!

She scowled and he grinned. That's when she realized he wasn't smiling over his bossy commands or the fact she'd slept the morning away. Aurora touched her head and groaned. Her hair was a rat's nest. "Don't look at my bedhead."

"Too late." He pointed to the tray he'd set on the table. "Poached courage, dry wheat toast—which is so disgusting—side of berries and orange juice no pulp, coffee with cream and sugar."

The man was too much. "Thank you."

"And a chocolate croissant because you deserve it. It's gonna be a long day. I let you sleep as late as I could. I debated on waking you for church, but after being blasted out of a building, I thought you might need the extra rest."

"Did you rest?"

He grinned. "I went to church. Wilder stayed next door."

"But…" She let the complaint drop. She had needed the extra rest. She wasn't a former navy SEAL.

"How do you feel?" he asked.

"Sore and miserable." Partly pain and partly because she'd thought he might kiss her last night, but he hadn't. She shouldn't be miserable and sore over that. It wouldn't be smart. But she was, nonetheless. Plus her head still hurt and her ears hadn't stopped ringing.

"Perfect. I'll leave you to it. Eat every bite." He winked and closed the door before she could protest. Instead, she sipped her coffee, which perked her up minimally.

She dressed and they traveled back to Richfield. Darla didn't have any more information than before, and Linda denied ever doctoring books nor did she admit any knowledge of Gus's shady business ethics. Beckett wasn't buying it, but Aurora believed them. Gus had hidden things well.

After the two failed questionings, they picked up the boxes at her childhood home. Mom hadn't noticed her wounds or asked about the case, but it hadn't upset Aurora like it used to. She wasn't going to feel guilty over that anymore. She'd even kissed Mom's cheek and told her she loved her. Something she hadn't done in a decade. Didn't matter that she'd barely registered the act or responded. Aurora was making changes. Doing the right thing even if feelings weren't reciprocated. She couldn't be responsible for everyone's actions. She had to be responsible for her own. And if she did the right thing, that would be enough.

No more guilt over outcomes she couldn't control. She was going to trust and follow God's orders like she expected those she advocated for to do.

Now they were ten minutes outside of Hope. "You want to go over these after we eat dinner?" Aurora asked.

Beckett popped a butterscotch candy. "I need to run home. I could cook something and we can sort through the boxes at my place. Change of scenery."

"You cook?"

"I surely do."

"Are you a decent cook?"

"I surely am."

She chuckled. "Then fix me dinner."

In twenty minutes, Beckett swung into his garage. Nice ranch-style house. He grabbed the boxes and motioned for Aurora to go inside first. Masculine kitchen. Dark wood trim. Earth tones. He placed the boxes on the kitchen table. "So, welcome to my house."

She kicked off her shoes. "What are you going to cook?"

"You like homemade pizza?"

"I like any kind of pizza," she said as she removed a lid from one of Richie's boxes. Tears stung her eyes. Photos of them playing in the yard. Richie's baseball photos. So many memories.

Beckett laid a hand on hers. "You want me to help with this?"

"No. You make pizza. But thanks for asking."

He opened up the fridge, pulling out ingredients.

"Did they never go through Richie's things?" Beckett asked as he kneaded dough.

"Yes, in his room. And his apartment after he went to prison. Guess they overlooked the shed." She dug through magazines, baseball cards, books on motorcycles and muscle cars. The smell of garlic, tomatoes and onions pierced the atmosphere. Aurora had never had a man cook for her before. She could get used to this.

"You like sausage and pepperoni?"

"I like whatever's edible." Aurora pulled out a wooden box. "This one is locked." She rummaged around for a key while Beckett sniffed the sausage, then plopped it in the heated skillet.

He glanced up. "You find a key?"

"Not yet." She dug deeper. "That smells amazing." After several minutes she frowned. "No key. I wonder what's in here."

"I don't know." Beckett finished topping the pizzas with the sausage, pepperoni, cheese and mushrooms, then wiped his hands on a towel and grabbed the box. "It's not a big lock. Hmmm... give me a second." He went into the garage and came back inside. "When all else fails, pick the stupid thing." He slid a small screwdriver-type object into the lock and turned.

It clicked.

"You do the honors."

"Is there anything you can't do?" Aurora marveled at Beckett's many abilities.

"I don't bake." He winked and Aurora opened the box.

She riffled inside. "Photos."

"Well, well, well. How 'bout that?" Beckett held the photo. Gus with his arm around Linda Wilcott, his sister-in-law, and it wasn't a very sisterly photo. The next one was of him pecking her neck.

"She sure didn't mention this little nugget when we talked with her earlier today."

No, she did not. This was a game changer.

"If these photos are hidden here, then is it possible Richie had this hanging over Gus's head? In order to get his money back?" Beckett asked.

"Maybe when Gus wouldn't give him the money owed, Richie threatened to go to Darla—or he did go to Darla. This gives her motive."

"And opportunity. Of course she never believed it was Richie. She knew she'd killed Gus and by garnering your sympathy, she could keep you close," Beckett added.

"She's still tight with Linda. She was on the phone with her that first day we visited. If she knew her sister had an affair with her husband, why keep contact with her but kill him?" Aurora frowned and flipped through the other photos.

"Keeping up appearances. Maybe she killed him and so, not to get caught, never mentioned it to Linda. To get off scot-free."

Whoa. More pictures of Linda and Gus, but also pictures of Gus and other women. "Is that a poker table in the background? Could he have been having affairs and using secret poker games as a cover to meet them? Right across the street from his wife!"

Beckett cocked his head. "I'm not sure what's going on, but someone might have caught Richie taking photos of Gus in compromising situations and thought he had photos of them, too. Framing Richie would get him out of the picture, so to speak, and Gus, too. Two birds. One stone."

"We should rattle some cages and throw out there we have photos from the private games. Be bait." Aurora laid the photos on the table.

"I don't like the idea of you putting yourself out there in that way."

"I'm already a target."

Beckett rubbed his chin. "Let's talk with Linda without Darla around. Lick that calf over again."

"Agreed. I'm not satisfied with our little talk with her, either. Not after seeing these photos."

"If Linda knows we have evidence that proves she had an affair, it might jog her memory about the books being doctored like Richie always claimed. If we hold this over her head…"

Aurora shook her index finger. "She might spill some hidden beans."

"And we'll climb the beanstalk all the way to the killer."

Beckett enjoyed watching Aurora eat the pizza. Enjoyed the whole night. The laughter. The discussion, though most of it concerned their circumstances. It was nice being in a home together. Having dinner. And she wore her hair down again.

Probably to hide some of her abrasions. He wasn't complaining. He loved it spilling down her back.

"That was the best pizza ever." Aurora wadded up her napkin. "And it was a breath of fresh air to get out of the inn for a while."

"I agree." He chuckled and carried her plate to the dishwasher. "You want another glass of tea?"

"No thanks." She grabbed her phone. "I'm gonna call Linda Wilcott. Set up another meeting. And since I know you want to be there—"

"Magnets."

"Yes, magnets. What day is good for you?"

"Probably Wednesday, after the Valentine's Day dance. Which reminds me, my mom has invited us to dinner tomorrow night. That work for you?"

"If you fill me in on what I can and can't say. I assume, since the explosion, she's aware I'm not staying home but at the inn." She gave him a pointed look.

"I didn't want her to worry."

"Good moms worry. It's what they do. She'd worry if you were a librarian." Aurora thumbed through the files she'd brought along and paused. "I can't believe Darla might have killed Gus. And is involved in all that's happening to me."

"She might not be." He finished cleaning up the dishes and put the leftover pizza in the fridge.

"I don't see Darla setting a bomb. I see Renzetti's goon doing that."

"What if Darla hired someone? A man attacked you. A man made the phone calls. She isn't doing this alone. She could easily know what was going on down here with the case, thanks to news media and social media. She could have researched you. One Google search and everything she needed would be at her fingertips. I hate Google," he teased.

Aurora snorted.

"At this point, everyone is a person of interest. Everyone has a motive. And opportunity." He raked a hand through his hair. "As far as my mom. She knows what's going on."

"And?"

Beckett opened the cabinet, dug around and came to the table, sitting across from Aurora. "She's glad we're in one piece." He handed her a Hershey's miniature bar. "Dessert."

Aurora snatched it. "I think I might be the only person to have actually gained weight during a major crisis in their life." She opened it up, inhaled the sweetness and broke it in half. "You wanna share it with me?"

"Absolutely." He'd share whatever he could. Yes, Mama was glad they were okay, but she'd gone on and on about how he could have died and that she thought he was past those life-threatening situations.

These days a traffic stop could be life threatening. But she deserved peace and joy in her life. Beckett hadn't even mentioned the offer in Atlanta again when Mama had brought up Wilder being in town. There was no point. Not after the way she'd fussed over him at the hospital yesterday.

Aurora handed him a piece of the chocolate. "I kept the bigger half."

"I *let* you take it," he countered with a hint of playfulness.

The stink eye he was coming to love about her flashed, but she refrained from commenting. She held up her cell phone. "So, I'll set it up for Wednesday."

"Make it somewhere other than Richfield. I don't want Darla getting wind of it."

"I have a feeling when we tell Linda we've found some interesting photos of her and Gus, she won't breathe a word to Darla about our meeting." Aurora made the call and Linda agreed to meet with them at a café about twenty minutes from Richfield.

A chill swept up Beckett's spine and he sat at attention.

"What is it?" Aurora asked.

"I'm not sure." He slowly stood and wandered toward the cabinets.

That's when he saw it.

"Stay there." He hustled from the kitchen into the living room, where he'd laid his coat. Grabbing his Glock, he hurried to his bedroom and out the door that led to a patio. He tiptoed to the edge of the house silently, listening.

Someone was on his property.

Watching.

The crunching of dead grass tipped him off to the trespasser's location. He moved with stealth toward the front yard.

A shadowed figure, in black, hunched near Beckett's car.

He picked up speed and snapped a twig in the dark.

The figure's head popped up and he bolted.

Beckett gave chase. Across his neighbor's yard and down the street until whoever had been hiding disappeared into the woods.

What had that person been doing? Watching? Planning another attack? Loosening Beckett's lug nuts? Planting a bomb? He jogged back and checked the tires. Everything was in place.

Inside, Aurora paced the kitchen. "Where did you go? What happened?"

"We were being watched. I lost whoever it was about a mile down the road and into the woods."

Aurora balled her fists, her voice shaky. "We're not safe anywhere, are we?"

No. Unfortunately, they weren't. Which meant he was going to need to take a few drastic measures. He bounded to his bag by the couch and took out a plastic box Wilder had purchased for him. Then he retrieved a black velvet box. "I was going to give you this on Valentine's." The dance was coming up and Beckett had to be there, which meant Aurora had to be with him. He hadn't had a chance to even discuss it yet.

"You bought me a Valentine's Day gift?" Aurora stood gaping.

His blood raced through his veins as he studied her surprised and confused expression. "Yes and no. This is all messed up. Not the way I wanted to do this. You know what? Just open it."

She stared at the long rectangular box. "When did you have time to shop for gifts?"

"I have my ways." He handed it to her. He'd seen the jewelry in the window at the Bless Her Heart Boutique. On impulse he'd purchased it and then freaked out. The last item of jewelry he'd bought was Meghan's engagement ring. That's when he got the other idea. And here he was.

Aurora shook her head. "Someone was just playing Peeping Tom and you want to give me a gift."

"No. I wanted to give it to you on Valentine's, but it's necessary now so…open it." She'd understand the urgency in a moment. It wasn't only a gift, though it had been when he'd first laid eyes on it, and then he ordered a few extra pieces online.

Aurora pursed her lips.

He shook his head. "*Please*, open it."

"See how nice simple gestures like 'please' can be." She cracked open the box and gasped. "Oh, Beckett, it's gorgeous." Turmoil swam across her face. She ran her hands over it, as if it were a treasure holding a promise she couldn't hang on to. In a sense, he supposed it was.

Inside the box lay a silver bracelet with three charms: the scales of justice in gold, a sterling silver chicken and a bronze egg.

"It's a charm bracelet. You can add to it." He removed it from the box. "Let me." He placed it on her delicate wrist. "You like it?"

"I love it," she said so heartbreakingly he almost threw caution to the wind and kissed her, demanding they discount all the reasons they couldn't move forward, but the devastation on her face kept his words and actions in check. He might be able to convince her. And then he'd break them both when they realized it was futile, but he wished things were different.

"A little inside joke," he said.

"Exactly." She studied it until recognition hit. "Oh! The egg's a locket."

Beckett nodded and marveled at the way surprise made her even more beautiful. "Which facilitates the need to give it to you now." He opened the other box and removed a small GPS tracker. "Precautionary, of course." He explained the device. "It tracks through a global satellite. So I won't lose a signal. I've already synced it with a device I can carry in my pocket." He placed the small chip inside the bronze egg locket. "Don't take it off."

"Sir, yes, sir." But she beamed. "It's thoughtful. Thank you. No one's ever bought me jewelry before."

How could that be possible? Well, he was glad to be the first. The thought of not being the last left him with a sour aftertaste.

"Or given me a GPS tracker to locate my every move." She snickered.

"I want to cover all my bases, keep you safe, Aurora." He skimmed the bracelet, letting his fingers brush her skin. "Have you thought about what you're going to do now that Kelly's…gone?"

"Do you mean will I stay on as court-appointed attorney? I guess that will be up to the new judge, but I see no reason for them not to keep me on. Why?" She narrowed her eyes.

"I'm not asking you to quit. Don't get all accusatory." But he wondered if she would. Selfish. Terrible thought. They both felt called to their careers. At some point, she'd meet a man who was on her side of the law or not involved in any side and he'd be placing jewelry on her wrist… her finger. He balled his fist and held back the pain and jealousy. He should have never bought the added charms. He was getting too emotional, losing focus. "I was just curious what the next step for you was."

"I'm going to keep fighting and championing people who need expert counsel. And I'm going to do it until they tell me I can't." Her countenance fell and he regretted even asking. She'd been lit up like a Christmas tree ten seconds ago.

"We should probably go. It's late."

She collected what she could with her uninjured hand and trudged to the garage.

He loaded the backseat with the boxes and opened Aurora's door. Could he find some way to make this work? Was it truly hopeless? He drove back to the inn, mulling it over.

He escorted her into her room and walked to the door. When he glanced back her way, she was fingering her charms, the sweetest grin on her face.

Emotions he'd been trying to keep in check got the better of him.

He strode back over to her, startling her.

"Aurora, about Valentine's Day…"

"I don't think so," Aurora said. "I mean, we have a lot going on. Do we really need to take a pause to attend a dinner and dance?" Dancing in Beckett's arms would be excruciating, knowing she'd have to leave them when the song ended.

"For St. Jude? Yeah."

"I don't mean we shouldn't donate. We should."

Beckett moved closer. "I have to be there. Magnets. Remember."

"Oh." Heat filled her cheeks. "For a second I thought—I mean it's not a… Right. I jumped to conclusions. The bracelet."

He tipped up her chin. "You didn't jump. Be my Valentine, Counselor. Eat dinner with me." He searched her eyes, his voice turned husky. "Dance with me," he said as he made his way strategically to her lips, revealing a tenderness she'd yet to discover about him. Her heart sprinted as he made his case with nothing but the elegance of his mouth and a feathered touch to her cheeks, the taste of butterscotch lingering on his lips.

His closing argument came when he slid his arm around her waist and lightly tugged her against him, proving she'd fit wholly and completely in his arms, that he was more than able to lead on the dance floor as skillfully and confidently as he led this perfectly perfect kiss.

She all but puddled to the floor when he broke it, his forehead resting against hers. "Say yes, Aurora. Say you'll come as my Valentine."

A war raged within her—her emotional side screaming yes, they'd find a way to make this work, and the logical side of her brain telling her that it was asinine to think it, and she wasn't a fling kind of girl and Beckett Marsh wasn't a fling kind of guy.

"Beckett..." She tried to resist.

"You're right. I didn't ask. I'll ask." He pecked her nose with such affection she wanted to die. But one of them had to keep their wits about them. It killed her it had to be her this time. And the fact he was going to *ask*. That he'd caught his mistake in demanding and was reversing it only made her want to cave and ignore the immovable mountain between them.

If he hadn't been standing right here, his nose pressed against hers, she'd collapse and cry, and she'd never cried over a man. A boyhood crush in sixth grade? Yes. But never a man because she'd never been in love until Beckett Marsh. How could she have let this happen?

"No. Please don't ask." She couldn't stand it. "It has to be no," she offered with a cracked voice, and broke away from the physical contact searing her. She turned to the wall. "We're both adults. We're smart. Where is this really gonna lead, Beckett?" She waited to see if he had a solution she hadn't thought of already. After several beats, she faced him. Did he have answers that she couldn't muster?

"I don't know." Hopelessness surfaced in his deliciously wonderful brown eyes.

That's what she'd been afraid of all along. "We

both know trying to make a go of something won't last but a blink of an eye. You're going to arrest people and I'm going to walk in and do what I do. We'll fight more than we won't."

"We haven't been fighting these past few days."

"What's going on now isn't day-to-day life. It's a bizarre situation, at best." A headache was coming on. "I'm simply trying to be realistic. And what if you move to Atlanta?"

"I'm not. I won't." The plea in his voice made a direct impact. Whether he stayed or left…it had to be for him. Why did he not realize that?

"I can't be a reason that you stay. I respect that you're factoring in your mother's feelings about keeping you close and safer. But guilt over that also shouldn't be a deciding factor. And, honestly… Meghan shouldn't be one, either."

"It isn't about Meghan."

Good. "What about your mom?"

"It's not guilt. It's respect. Honor. Love."

All things Aurora loved about him. And all the reasons they were dead in the water. They might have a fighting chance if he left the state. But not if he stayed, and she wasn't going to push him to leave for her. If he went, it had to be as an asset to Wilder's team and right for Beckett.

Which put them back at square one.

She wasn't quitting.

Beckett wasn't, either.

"You know, according to the magnet analogy, I have to go, but this dance is nothing more than a fairy tale with a bad ending. At least acknowledge you know it." She lost her breath from the ache. The room closed in on her. Would he admit it? Could he? He seemed to press for what he couldn't have. One of them had to be reasonable, no matter how much it hurt.

"Let's get some rest. We need it." Beckett changed the subject. It was clearly over and done with. He pivoted at the door. "I know you're right. For a minute, I didn't care. I'm sorry. It won't happen again," he said.

"If things were different—"

"I lost my head."

She'd lost her heart.

"Good night, Counselor." He gave her an equally forlorn expression and disappeared behind the door.

Another barrier keeping them apart.

TWELVE

Beckett looked in the mirror and flicked his spiky bangs, frowning. He should have shaved, but he'd kept the scruff to cover a few scratches from the explosion Saturday. It felt like more than a few days had passed. More like two months. And yet it seemed as if it was only last night he'd been in Aurora's room, heady from kissing her. Wishing to stay locked in that embrace.

He opted for a crisp white shirt with a black suit jacket. He straightened his black silk tie, then undid it and tossed it on the chair, leaving the top two buttons undone to breathe. Ties were meant for funerals or weddings. Not Valentine's Day dates. Except this wasn't a date. Aurora had voiced the truth he already knew deep down. Closing the door on her that night had closed the door on their chances. He *had* lost his head.

She wasn't moving. He wasn't moving, though he'd thought a lot about Atlanta these past few days. But what would happen if he became emotionally invested in a case while working with Wilder? What would he do? He could never let himself get back to the dark place like when Meghan died. When he'd almost killed Parker Hill.

But could he stay in this town and watch Aurora eventually fall for another man? He didn't want to think about it. He had a case to work. To laser in on.

The SWAT bomb commander had told him that his findings were inconclusive. Most likely it was the same explosives guy Franco Renzetti used, but there were enough contrasts in style that it could have been copycatted to appear like a hit by Renzetti. He confirmed what Beckett had been thinking. If anyone had discovered the signature the bomber used when crafting explosive devices, hundreds of online videos gave tutorials on how to create a bomb. Not to mention anyone could have hired someone to set it. It was as easy as putting an ad in the classifieds or an online sales paper.

So it could have been Darla or her son, Little Gus. Or even Linda. She might have offed Gus to keep Darla from finding out about their affair. She could have hired someone.

But he still couldn't let Oliver slip away. He'd left town but wasn't scheduled to go back to work, so who knew where he was at the moment. Coming to apologize at this time in Aurora's life—yeah, tomorrow was the anniversary of his son's death—but it didn't feel right. Where was he?

And lastly, Franco Renzetti. The bomb made sense. The other threats and attacks, he couldn't be 100 percent sure.

But Oliver.

It kept coming back to the attorney.

Beckett had been over it a hundred times. He had barely heard what Pastor Bradley said Sunday in church. Between figuring out who might be after Aurora and being distracted by thoughts of Aurora in general, he might have picked out a few of the verses.

Lord, don't hold back Your tender mercies from me. Let Your unfailing love and faithfulness always protect me.

He'd perked up at that Scripture and made it his own prayer over himself and Aurora. They needed protecting and with Wilder now gone, Beckett was her sole guardian. But he was only a man. And men made mistakes. Men didn't make it in time every time. Men were flawed.

He'd proven that.

Shaking the nerves from his hands, he knocked on Aurora's door.

She opened it, knocked the breath from him.

Stunning.

She wore a long-sleeved black dress that touched

the top of her knees. She'd left her hair long, and it flowed in shiny waves. Sparkly earrings dangled from her ears. On her good hand, she wore the charm bracelet. He hoped it was out of love for the gift and not just the GPS tracker.

"You look…amazing. I was going to bring flowers—just so you know I'm not a jerk. But after our conversation—"

"I don't think you're a jerk, Beckett."

Even if he had brought a bouquet, it wouldn't hold a candle to her.

"Let me grab my purse." She hurried back inside, a pro on those super high heels. They'd brought her nearly to his nose. After she grabbed it and a shawl of some sort, he escorted her from the inn. "It's freezing out."

The low was in the twenties tonight; already the temperature was dropping. "I'm seriously considering moving to the Bahamas." He opened the door for her and helped her into the car, then darted around to the driver's side.

He cranked the engine and caught her gawking at him. His chest swelled. "What?" But he knew she was admiring him.

"You look good, Mr. Bond."

"I am packin' a weapon or two." He patted his side and drove them to Mitch Rydell's. Dozens of vehicles were already parked, and smooth, romantic music sounded from inside the barn. How was he going to make it through this night? "You mind keeping my keys in your purse?"

"Sure." She dropped them in her clutch. "I like your car, by the way."

"I didn't want to be the sheriff tonight." Lately, he didn't want to be the sheriff at all. He'd been wrestling with what Aurora had said about him being content and happy. He'd been trying to convince himself all along that he was. That this was the right thing, staying in Hope. He was fulfilling the Scripture he'd carried in his wallet after Meghan died. Yet, he squirmed inside. Completely unsettled.

The authorities are God's servants, sent for your good. But if you are doing wrong, of course you should be afraid, for they have the power to punish you. They are God's servants, sent for the very purpose of punishing those who do what is wrong.

He'd taken that note to punish entirely out of context, justifying his sin as he hunted down Parker Hill.

Had he really come here after Meghan for a fresh start? Just to take care of Mama?

No. He'd been afraid of falling off the edge again. He'd been hiding. Maybe that's why he recognized it in Aurora when she'd moved here. She'd mirrored him.

He blew a heavy breath and scanned his surroundings.

Clear-bulb lights hung from the rafters and walls, creating a soft glow. Rustic lanterns with candles burning inside sat on tables with white tablecloths. Tin buckets held spring flowers, and a stage had been created for the live band.

Several people waved. Some whispered. No doubt wondering if he and Aurora were an item, and if so, how long it could last. Didn't they basically fight for two different things? Some even scowled as if he were fraternizing with the enemy.

They didn't know Aurora like he did. They didn't understand her view. What drove her. They didn't see the compassionate woman willing to risk her own life to help others.

Speaking of lives, Johnna waved and blew Aurora a kiss. She could have blown up in that explosion if it hadn't been for Aurora.

He led her with his hand on the small of her back, noticing how well it fit there. They found their table in the corner. Placards with their names had been laid out for them.

"Do you feel awkward?" Aurora asked. "I'm not blind. People have been talking for days. Speculating that something is going on between us."

He helped her out of her coat, thankful for the

heated barn. "I never was a fan of rumors and gossip." The only thing going on between them was pure misery. "Let's get a drink. Sparkling cider?"

She nodded and they made their way to the drink table.

"Aurora, you're lovely."

Beckett admired Mama. Always classy. "You're lovely, yourself."

"Yes, Virginia, you do look beautiful," Aurora said.

She beamed. "I think this is the most gorgeous event we've done yet. Mitch's stable hands are doing carriage rides through the pasture. No snow, but it's still wonderful."

"That sounds fun." Aurora sipped her cider and let her gaze wander over the barn.

Beckett should have offered to take her. But snuggling under a quilt, that close to her lips—and after a kiss that had been mind-blowing—it was smarter to keep his distance. Focus on the case.

The next hour they spent mingling with friends, acquaintances and those simply curious about what the sheriff was doing on a perceived date with the defense attorney. Holt McKnight caught his attention and motioned for him.

"Hey, man. How are things?"

Beckett groaned. "I'm chasing rabbits, dude. It could be anyone. At this point, maybe it's all of them. They've formed some sort of I Hate Aurora Daniels club and they're all coming after her."

Holt clucked his tongue inside his cheek. "Doubtful," he deadpanned. "Who has the most to gain by wiping her out?"

Beckett downed his cider and scanned the room for Aurora. She was in the corner talking to Mitch. He grunted.

Holt followed his line of sight and clasped his shoulder. "Get a grip."

"I know. I know. But they'd work. She could easily be with him and no one would question his integrity. She could continue doing what she loves for a living." *He could buy her all sorts of jewelry.* His temperature rose. "And if I'm being honest, I hate the idea, but I want her to be happy. Not have to deal with so many complications. I also want to knock Mitch Rydell through the barn wall."

Holt raised his eyebrows. Glad he found this amusing. There was nothing amusing about it.

"If you love her, Beck, *make* it work. End of story. From a man who knows." Holt raised his glass and left Beckett alone.

Easier said than done.

Aurora caught his eye, mirroring the same tortured expression he felt. She lifted her cider glass in response, then broke eye contact, as if seeing him pained her.

It pained him.

He couldn't stand here all night and watch Aurora and Mitch. He wasn't actually going to toss him through the wall, but having the fleeting thought scared him. He couldn't go over the edge. He refused.

Taking his mind off it, he talked with townsfolk. Casual conversations. No one dared ask him about Aurora, other than if she was okay after the café exploded. Some asked if he had any leads on who had done such a horrible thing. He gave a standard response: "We don't have any conclusive answers, but we're doing everything we can to find who did this and bring him to justice."

He only hoped when he did discover who was behind terrorizing and attempting murder on Aurora he'd keep his wits about him. He finally strode to the corner of the room, but Aurora was no longer with Mitch.

"Hey, Sheriff. You enjoying yourself?"

Not so much. "Where's Aurora?" Beckett asked.

Mitch pointed outside the barn. "Cell rang and she said she had to take it."

"Thanks." He strode outdoors. People milling about in conversation.

No Aurora.

His phone rang. Wilder.

"Hey, man."

"Hey. While I was doing a more extensive search, like you asked the other day, I found some interesting information on Linda Wilcott and Darla McGregor."

Beckett paused. "What's that?"

"They have a brother. And he did time. He was let out about eight months ago."

A brother was never mentioned. "What was he in for?"

"Well, he belonged to a small antigovernment commune. He got picked up for assault and battery, but the crazies he lived with had enough weapons for a small militia. Including a truckload of C-4 and other materials that could be used to construct a bomb."

Beckett's gut churned. The brother would have access to materials if he was still in contact with commune members. "You locate him?"

"Oh, yeah. He's living with his nephew. Gus McGregor Jr."

"Little Gus." The brother could have easily acted on behalf of either one of his sisters. Dropped the engine. Attacked them. Set the bomb. "Thanks." He hung up and hurried around the barn in time to be accosted by a figure.

Aurora smacked her phone. "I can't hear you. You're cutting out on me."

Linda Wilcott had phoned her, hysterical. But Aurora couldn't get a clear connection out here.

"Miss Daniels. Can you hear me now?"

Aurora poked a finger in her ear at the shoddy reception. "Yes. I can. Say that again." She moved closer to Mitch's driveway at the main house.

"After we talked on the phone the other day about those photos you found, it was obvious you knew about me and Gus. I decided to go to Darla and let her hear it from me first. But when I told her today she said she already knew. She ranted about all of Gus's infidelities and that I was another victim of his—which isn't true—but it scared me. I think she might have done something real bad. I found something from her garage you should see. I think it's the murder weapon."

Aurora clutched her chest. Darla had known and killed Gus as some kind of saving mission to rescue her sister from him. But to frame Richie? To let him go to prison?

People can fall fast. Beckett's words came back around. Grief. Pain. It could change a person, and not for the better. "Where are you now?" Darla might come after Linda.

"I'm actually on Farley Pass. My car stalled out."

Had someone tampered with her vehicle, too? Little Gus? Darla herself?

"If she finds out I have this…I wanted to get out of town. Get it to you as soon as possible."

She turned toward the barn. "I can come get you. Take you to the sheriff's station."

"Okay. Hurry," she said in a shaky voice.

Aurora hung up and went on a search for Beckett. Where was he? Most of the night he'd been keeping a watchful eye on her. The whole evening had been an emotional disaster. So many couples enjoying the romantic atmosphere. Shared looks, touches, kisses. All the things she wanted with Beckett.

A commotion sounded from the side of the barn where several bales of hay and a generator-powered heater made for a warm sitting area.

Someone screeched.

Aurora stopped at the edge of the barn. Beckett was restraining someone. She squinted.

Quent Russell.

He swung at Beckett, clipping his jaw. "You know what she did! And you're making it with her!"

Oh, my. Aurora's face heated as a few eyes made contact with hers, some embarrassed, some questioning and some accusing.

Not noticing Aurora in the dark, Beckett sprang forward in a span of seconds, pinning Quent on the ground, face in the dirt. "Son, watch your mouth, for one. You don't talk about ladies like that. Secondly, you need to cool off sooner rather than later." Beckett scanned the crowd of spectators. "Anybody seen his daddy?"

"My daddy ain't here! I saw you and her. At your house!"

Well, that explained the lurker in the yard that night.

"My mom would roll over in her grave knowing you would take up with—"

Beckett hauled Quent up by his jacket collar. *"That's it."*

Aurora spotted Blair and rushed to her, not wanting to put herself in Quent's vicinity. "Give these to Beckett. He'll need them to take Quent Russell home." She gave Blair the keys.

"Hey, not everybody feels that way. Quent's hurting."

"I'm not stupid. I know Beckett and I can't have anything more than friendship. It's a nice thought, though."

"That's not true."

"Don't argue with me, Blair. I'm a trial lawyer." She left the keys and hurried to find Mitch.

"Hey, Mitch! Can I borrow your car? Beckett has his hands full and I need to pick up a friend who's stranded." Every second counted. She was only a few minutes away. Once she picked up Linda, she'd go straight to the sheriff's station. She'd be safe. They both would.

"You need me to take you?" Mitch asked.

"No, I'm fine." No sense dragging more people into this. "If you don't mind me borrowing a vehicle."

"Nah, if you don't mind driving a pickup." He handed her the keys to his silver Ford F-150.

She hopped in. "Thanks." After buckling up, she sent Beckett a text:

Gone to pick up Linda Wilcott at Farley Pass. Car broke down. You had hands tied with Quent. Meet us at station. Borrowed Mitch's truck.

She laid on the gas and headed for Linda. Could Darla have lied straight to Aurora's face like that? Clients did it all the time. So, yeah, she could have.

"Lord, help me. Help me clear Richie's name. Then help me to know what the next step is." She saw Linda's car on Farley Pass. She pulled to the edge of the road and rolled down her passenger window. "Hey, Linda! Get in."

Linda hurried to the truck and climbed in. Her hair was in disarray and her pupils were dilated, eyes shifty.

"Are you feeling all right?"

"Yeah. Yeah. Just freaked-out, you know?"

"Right." Aurora edged onto the road and made her way toward the sheriff's station. "Tell me what happened."

Linda shook her head. "It was a huge mistake,

me and Gus, but I loved him. Long before Darla ever even met him!" Her tone grew louder, and a strange sensation skittered along Aurora's skin.

"So you confessed you'd had an affair and Darla admitted she knew?"

"She did. She said awful things about Gus. Said he seduced me like the others. Seduced me so I'd cook his books. But I never did that. I mean, I did fudge a few things. Lessened some of the hours the guys worked when Gus was in a financial mess."

So Linda had contributed to Richie being ripped off. Gus had owed him more money for the hours he'd billed on cars. But Linda had adjusted the time cards and logs and Richie could never prove it. "Did Gus have you do that?"

"No…well…yes, but he said the men were lying. They were hoodwinking him out of hours."

And Linda had believed him because she was in love with him.

"Your sister knew all this and never confronted you?"

"No. But she confronted Gus. She said she'd handled it and to keep my mouth shut." Tears streaked her cheeks. "I went to digging in the garage after that and I found this." She pulled out a clear storage bag encasing a wrench. In the dark, Aurora wasn't sure if that was blood or rust on it. "What are we gonna do?"

"First you're going to tell Sheriff Marsh all this at the station and then he can have some testing done. DNA. Fingerprints. Then we'll question Darla."

"You can't."

"Why?" Aurora turned left.

"Because she's reckless right now. I think she might even be suicidal. She could be taking her life as we speak."

The hysteria in Linda's voice sent a wave of panic through Aurora. "How do you know that? And if that's true, why didn't you call the police?"

"I did."

"You called the police and then left?" Something wasn't adding up.

"I was afraid to stay, but I don't want to see my sister hurt herself." She shoved the bag back into her purse, keeping her hands inside. Then she let out a frightening cry. "I don't want to do this."

Aurora's grip tightened on the wheel. "You don't want to do what?"

"You haven't given me a choice, Aurora! Cops will start searching my place. I have to do this." Linda pulled a gun from her bag, pointing it directly at her. "Keep driving."

Aurora's blood raced through her veins, leaving her light-headed.

"Linda, what's going on? Have you done all

this to me? Because I'm trying to exonerate my innocent dead brother?"

"I—I— Just drive!"

"Is that the real murder weapon or were you using it as a decoy?" Was she trying to save Darla? Was Darla on her way out of town or something? Or was Linda trying to save herself? The pieces wouldn't fit into place.

"I have to bury it somewhere new. Somewhere far away from me and my house. I don't know! I can't keep it."

Linda was going off half-cocked here. Had she thought anything through? Or was she reacting out of panic now? "Where? Where are we heading, Linda?"

"Your place. Go to your place, and don't you dare try anything or I'll…I'll shoot you right here and now."

Irrational. Erratic. Aurora needed to think. *Be calm.* Assert authority without being intimidating. She turned left, heading to her house. "Linda, I thought you said Darla killed Gus. Did she?"

"He was going to leave her. He was." She wiped her nose on the sleeve of her coat.

Be calm. She searched the roads. Could she wreck them and get away? "Why didn't he leave her, Linda? What happened that night? Did you see Richie?"

Linda wrung her hands. "I never saw Richie.

I knew Gus was working late. Thought I'd surprise him but...when I showed up, he was in the garage. With Darla. He was with her. And I knew he'd been lying to me. Seducing me."

"Darla told you that."

Deep lines creased her forehead as she squinted. "Darla? No. Darla didn't know."

"But you said that you confessed to Darla and she told you she'd known all along and handled it. You said she's suicidal right now." Aurora came to a four-way stop and turned right. Once they arrived at her home, she might have the upper hand due to familiarity.

"Stop trying to confuse me!" she hollered, and shoved the gun into her temple. "Drive."

"I'm trying to understand, Linda. Are you telling me that *you* killed Gus?" She worked to make sense of everything Linda was spewing. "I can help you. I'm a defense attorney." Would she? No way. But she needed Linda to lower that gun before it went off accidentally. She needed to do whatever she had to in order to survive.

"You're lying!"

"I *can* help you. You could tell a judge you're not in your right mind. Not now or back then when you realized Gus had been using you to fix the books. Which is what he did, wasn't it, Linda? He used you."

Linda let a wail escape her lips. "He did. And

I told him so, but he didn't care. So I…I got so mad, you know. I blinked and he was lying there, bleeding and not moving."

"You hit him with the wrench. The wrench you brought?" Why would she bring it?

"Yes. Then I ran. I went home, hid it and I kept my mouth shut. I was scared. But now the cops will be coming and I have to get it far away from me, from Richfield, where no one will think to look."

Why not throw it in the Mississippi? Aurora could think of a dozen places better than here. But Linda was panicked. Irrational. And impulsive.

"Does Darla know now what you did?"

Linda kept silent.

"She never really confessed to anything, did she? Because she didn't know about you and Gus. You kept it quiet so you wouldn't get caught." Was Linda planning to kill Darla and pass it off as a suicide? She could have already murdered her.

Linda refused to speak, but the truth was written on her face. Aurora had hit the nail on the head.

"Linda…" She had to make one last effort.

"Shut up!"

Aurora approached her home and turned into the drive.

"I didn't want it to end this way. But you won't leave things alone. It was a long time ago! Get out."

Linda kept the gun trained on Aurora as she eased from the truck.

Carefully Aurora unlocked the door to her house, the gun poking into her ribs. "Are you going to shoot me in my own home, Linda?"

"I been keeping up with what's going on. Saw you raised a stink in the town over that boy. They'll find you dead and anyone can be to blame. The dead lady's husband. Anyone you made mad. Doesn't matter."

"Linda, think this through." Could she? The woman was off her rocker.

Linda used the gun to urge her into the house.

"Right now, you have a case. You could win it. Temporary insanity. You could plead out, do way less time, especially if you turn in the murder weapon instead of trying to rebury it somewhere else. But this...this is murder one, Linda. This will get you life. And Beckett will figure out the truth. You and I know that." He'd come straight for Linda.

She rubbed the bracelet on her wrist. When Beckett realized she wasn't at the station or coming, and wouldn't answer her phone, he could track her.

But would it be in time?

Aurora stood in the middle of the dark living room. Only a sliver of moonlight beamed upon

Linda. Wild-eyed and hand shaking, she kept the gun on Aurora.

"Linda, you don't have to do this. It won't work. Let me help you."

Aurora wasn't getting through to the woman.

"You didn't have to go to these lengths." Aurora paused. She didn't. A man had attacked her in her garage. A man had threatened her. "Who did you get to help you?"

Linda grabbed her head. "I can't think! Shut up! This is all your fault. Everything was fine. Just fine."

Pop!

Aurora hit the ground. Glass littered the floor where the bullet had sliced through the freshly fixed window. Linda collapsed, red staining her neck and chest.

Beckett! Beckett found her.

She trembled, then jumped up when the door creaked open farther.

"You don't know how glad I am to see you!" She rushed to the door and stopped dead in her tracks.

"What? Not happy to see me?"

Her knees turned to water. This couldn't be happening.

"You're dead. You died." She backed up a step. And another.

"Did I?" He tsked. "Don't believe everything you read or see on the news, Aurora."

Severin Renzetti stood before her. Gun in one hand. Shovel in the other.

THIRTEEN

"But how?" Aurora glanced toward the kitchen, planning an escape. Severin Renzetti had died in prison. Someone had put a hit out on him and he'd been shanked. Back in June.

"Aurora, I never took you to be dull-headed. When you have the kind of money and power I have, you can pay anyone off to say anything. Guards. Medical personnel. Funeral home directors. The list goes on. Everyone has a price."

He raised his gun. "Let's take a ride, shall we?"

She froze.

"Now," he boomed.

Aurora walked on jellylike legs through the front door. The scent from her office, the garage… same scent on Severin now. Same cologne he used to wear, unique. That's why she couldn't place it and yet it had felt familiar.

Severin had faked his death.

No vehicle out front but Mitch's.

"We'll take your friend's truck. Keys, please."

He held out his hand, a sickly-sweet smile on his face.

Where had he parked? Off on a back road? Down the street? Couldn't be too far. Aurora and Linda had only been inside for a few minutes before he'd killed her. She handed him the keys grudgingly.

He opened the passenger's side. "Get in." Reluctantly she climbed inside the cab and scooted to the driver's side, then he slid into the passenger seat, his gun trained on her. "Drive. Hope Lake."

Her hands shook as she cranked the engine. "You don't have enough money to pay people off forever. They'll want more. They'll eventually talk. They can't help themselves."

"Dead people don't talk, Aurora. You'll discover that soon enough." He grabbed her arm and forced her to look him in the eye. "Ask me what kept me going in prison."

She couldn't speak. Couldn't breathe.

He shook her. "Ask me!"

"What? What kept you going?" she squeaked.

"Revenge."

Aurora swallowed, but her mouth and throat were like sandpaper. He let her go and signaled with the gun to drive.

"You stole my life away from me. Everything I cared about."

So Severin was taking it all from her.

He forced her to park in the secluded lot at Hope Lake, and then he marched her into the dense woods, the chill already causing her teeth to chatter. Up a steep hill, where her heels sank into the ground, making it difficult to move, on top of the fact her body was freezing. She'd planned to be in a heated barn all night, not climbing a hill in the middle of the woods in twenty-degree weather.

"How long have you been out of prison?" she asked.

"Long enough to watch you settle in and act small-town. Long enough to know you riled up the good people of Hope," he mocked. "I'm a patient man. But you know this."

He'd made subtle advances toward her. She'd thwarted them all. And he'd told her: *Aurora, after this case is over you'll see I'm not my father. I'm a patient man. I can wait for you.*

"Long enough to see you get chummy with the sheriff. I thought I had him that day in the garage when I cut through the chain. I admit I would have liked to have seen him smashed. And you. But this, no, this is much better."

Severin had followed them and worked on cutting the chain while they interviewed Darla. He'd been watching them as they rode horses. When Beckett almost kissed her, he'd fired the gun. Jealousy, or was he simply enjoying his evil scheme? Either way, the thought nauseated her.

"It was you in the crowd that day, wasn't it?" She noticed the shovel again. Was he going to kill her and bury her out here? Would Beckett find her in time?

"It was."

"And the phone calls?"

"You put up a brave front. I enjoyed watching you sleep."

"Why Kelly? You murdered her."

"That's on you. I wouldn't have had to take her away from you. But you robbed me of people I care about."

Severin cared for no one but himself. She didn't utter a word, though.

He laughed and shoved her forward. She lost her balance and collapsed into the mud.

"You blew up my business. You knew I'd come fix that stupid machine. What is this? Plan B?" She worked to sound brave. Her knees knocked and her feet had gone numb. She could barely stand. Severin yanked her up.

"You blew up mine when the guilty verdict came in! But you're wrong, Aurora. I didn't know about that machine. I *have* learned that every Saturday your employees clean the machines. And that means unplugging them."

"I guess your dad hooked you up with his bomb guy." Aurora stumbled forward like a baby calf.

"I'm not discussing my dad. Unlike you, I protect the people I love. You won't even be able to save your new man."

"He'll end you."

Severin backhanded her. The sting blinded her as blood filled her mouth. "Move."

She continued to push farther into the woods, her teeth clicking together uncontrollably, but adrenaline raced to help her ignore the rawness of the elements. It seemed like they walked for miles. "What about Linda? You killed the only suspect."

"Get real, Aurora. The best suspect here is Oliver Benard. That crazy woman tried to take you out, but Benard has been planning your demise for too long to let anyone else have you first. He's been quietly lurking in the shadows. He saw her get in the truck with you at Farley Pass, but neither of you noticed him in the distance. He made his move. Shot her. Then he murdered you and maybe he killed himself because he couldn't take it."

How had she not realized Severin had been following her all this time? She hadn't seen any cars on the road earlier. "Is he dead? Is Oliver dead?" Aurora's blood drained from her head. "Have you murdered him, too?"

The moon slashed through the trees, and up ahead she saw a mound of dirt. Her stomach roiled and panic set off a spasm of shakes. "Severin...please..."

Before her lay a wooden box.

She blinked, shivered.

She stared down at the grave. He couldn't. She couldn't let him. Terror scorched her chest and tears welled.

"Found this nice secluded spot when I was following you and the sheriff on your little ride. Dug it days ago. But no way was I going to let Loony Linda get the glory of taking your life. That's unfair and wrong." He snarled, eyes glazing over. "Things seem to be looking up for me. Like you. You'll be looking up at me." He banged the shovel on the box. "Get in."

Tears poured down her cheeks. She couldn't control them. "No!"

"You let me rot in prison. Day after day. It's your turn, Aurora. To rot and think about what you did. You've been put on trial."

No.

"Final verdict? Guilty as charged. Get. In. That. Box."

Severin may have been plotting his revenge since he'd entered the prison system, but she was not going to bear that responsibility anymore. He belonged there.

But she couldn't get into that wooden grave. She sobbed and begged, but Severin shoved her toward it. Her calves hit the edge and she tripped, landing inside. He swung her throbbing legs into the box, splinters digging into her bare skin. The smell of pine and earth drenched her senses.

Beckett, find me.

She grabbed for her bracelet to give her some comfort that Beckett could track her.

Fear bulleted through her.

It was gone!

It must have broken and fallen off when Severin shoved her and she'd collapsed in the mud. But she couldn't be sure.

God, help him find me somehow! Please don't let me die this way.

The back of her head hit the wood. "Severin, I'm sorry. Please. Let me go and I won't say a word. I won't tell anyone you're alive. I promise."

"Like you said, people talk. They can't help themselves. And I'm enjoying myself."

"You're sick."

"Is that your closing argument? Because it was weak." His smug expression erased the charm and good looks, revealing nothing but his ugliness.

"I don't need a closing argument. Sentencing has clearly been passed."

"Fiery. I like that. Hey, at least when they see that crazy woman dead in your house and put the pieces together, everyone will know Richie never murdered anyone. You've accomplished what you set out to do. That ought to give you some solace while you rot in this wooden cell."

"You won't get away with this. Beckett will figure it out." But Beckett could only track her as far as the bracelet, and they'd moved up two hills and deeper into the woods. A mile, maybe even two—she couldn't be sure. And if she'd lost it in Mitch's truck, then it could be even farther.

The bitter weather seeped into her marrow, terror weaving through the wintry temperature. She couldn't feel her toes.

"He might. But I'll be long gone to a country where there's no extradition. And you'll be dead either way." He leaned down. "I wonder what will kill you first. Lack of oxygen or the elements." He laughed. "Enjoy prison, Aurora."

He closed the lid while she screamed and begged.

She was plunged into sheer darkness.

"Severin!" She pressed on the lid, hollering until her chest was on fire. Air. She needed to conserve her air and hope Beckett would figure out how to find her without her bracelet.

She heard a click. Then the box moved. She screamed as he lowered it into the grave.

The sound of dirt pelting on wood came over and over again as she silently cried and beat on the box, her eyes refusing to adjust. Uncontrollable tremors convulsed her body.

She was being buried alive.

* * *

Beckett had called a deputy to pick up Quent and take him home, then he'd searched for Aurora until Blair brought him the keys to his car. He went to call her and that's when he saw the text. Had Aurora lost her ever-loving mind?

When she didn't answer his call, he'd found Mitch, and he confirmed giving Aurora a vehicle. He'd also confirmed that he'd rented out other horses the day they took their ride. The shooter could have been Linda and Darla's brother. Beckett should have thought to ask then, but he'd failed.

Beckett had already left Farley Pass. But not before he'd checked Linda's car, which was in perfect condition. She'd lied. Had she and her brother taken Aurora?

He checked his tracking device. Aurora was at Hope Lake. He sped toward the lake, praying she was all right. That he'd be in time.

He hadn't been in time to save Meghan.

He couldn't catch a breath.

Why would Linda or her brother take Aurora out to the lake? Were they planning on drowning her and burying her at the bottom? Hadn't it crossed either of their demented minds that Aurora had already told Beckett they were on the way to the station? *Please, God, don't let me be too late. Help me find her.*

He pulled out his tracking device again. She

was about a mile from the lake's vacant parking lot. Not a single vehicle but Mitch's. The red blinking dot identifying Aurora's position wasn't moving. He might have a fighting chance if he booked it. He parked beside Mitch's truck.

Grabbing his flashlight, he set out to rescue Aurora.

His previous failure shone like blinding light in his brain.

Following the signal into the woods, he continued praying for her safety and that he'd make it in time. He couldn't let thoughts of failing Meghan interfere with his focus. But the fear that history was about to repeat itself distracted him.

Closer.

Closer.

Beckett stood with woods surrounding him on all sides. Aurora should be here. Somewhere. He ran the flashlight across the ground and attuned his ears, as well as his gut instinct.

Wind.

Dead leaves rustling along his feet.

No voices.

Something flashed near a muddy area. He inched forward and squatted.

Oh, no. No. No.

Lying in the mud was Aurora's bracelet.

A scuffle had taken place. "God," he whispered, "protect her." Time to call in backup.

No. Beckett was now going to have to do this the hard way. Track her without help from a global satellite. He'd done this several times on missions. Or as a boy hunting animals. A slew of deputies would trample brush and footprints. Their flashlights swiveling across the woods might draw attention and cause the killer to panic and become desperate.

He could move faster and safer for Aurora if he used his training and went alone.

But time wasn't on his side, and his past hovered like dense fog on the edges of his heart, his mind.

God, direct me. I can't do this on my own. I'm just a man. Lead me to her! Beckett had been working to resolve this in his heart and to find peace, knowing that while he hadn't been able to save Meghan, she'd known the Lord. She was in His arms now and safe—protected. Who knew why God saved and rescued some and others left this life? Either way, Beckett had to trust Him.

He set out, checking for cracked branches, footsteps, any sign of brush that had been pressed down from people trudging through it. He battled the darkness with only a single beam from his flashlight, but he moved fast, tracked and prayed continually—for guidance and Aurora's safety.

Beckett forced his pulse to slow. Focused on clearing the fog. He needed all his faculties, his senses. Continuing uphill, he followed the signs of people. Had to be Aurora; hikers would have a solid print, but a few he could make out had the point of a heel. She'd been in spiky heels.

Up ahead he spied a mound of earth.

His pulse spiked. No. No. No.

He barreled toward what looked like a fresh grave. He dropped to his knees and instantly clawed his way through the dirt.

"Aurora!"

No answer.

The trees bent and bowed at the heavy gusts of wind.

In her little dress, underground. On a night like this. How long had she been buried? He hadn't spotted anyone on his trek to find her. They'd hidden in the woods or bypassed him somehow. Right now that didn't matter.

Aurora alone mattered.

He frantically dug, a cold sweat seeping through the back of his shirt. His pulse thumped mercilessly in his temples. He couldn't have failed twice.

"Aurora! Can you hear me?" He raced against time, clawing…digging.

Would he be fast enough? An hour. It'd been a full hour since her text. Dirt clogged his nails and flew into his face, mouth, eyes.

"Aurora!" he continued to call, begging for her

to answer. Begging for her to be alive. Moisture filled his eyes as he worked and dug until his muscles burned, but he kept digging deeper. Each handful of dirt was a prayer that he was in time.

God, I can't save her. But You can. Forgive me for thinking I have that power. Please save her. They might never be together with the obstacles before them, but, God help him, he loved her and needed her to live.

He forged ahead, tirelessly clawing through the dirt, terrified he'd find a lifeless body, vacant blue eyes he'd come to adore.

A world no longer filled with Aurora Daniels.

Another spear to Beckett's side.

He finally struck something hard.

Wood.

He knocked on it. Called her name.

Nothing.

Hysteria ripped through his veins.

He stripped off his suit coat and used it to clear the remaining debris. The box was padlocked. His hair clung to his head.

His pick was back in the truck and there wasn't time.

He jumped from the shallow grave, frantically hunting for something to break the latch. Using his phone as a flashlight he found a large rock. Grabbing it, he ran back to the box holding Aurora and smacked it against the padlock.

Over and over again.

Until it gave way and fell from the latch. He flipped it open and let out a cry.

Aurora lay inside.

Unmoving.

Dirt and grime clung to her haggard skin, her lips a frightening shade of blue.

He lifted her onto the ground and checked for a pulse, her skin feeling rubbery. Frostbite.

Something hard smashed into the back of his head sending him face-first to the ground in a dizzy spell.

"I get back to Aurora's truck, and, lo and behold, look who's come to rescue her. Sorry, but I can't have you ruining my plans."

Beckett didn't recognize the voice. He gathered his bearings and rolled to his back as the man brought down a shovel toward his face.

Beckett flipped to the side, then grabbed the bottom of the tool, throwing the man off balance, giving Beckett time to jump to his feet and tackle him.

They fell to the ground, the man on his back.

That's when Beckett realized who he was facing. Severin Renzetti. But how? He was supposed to be dead.

Severin blazed with rage as he head-butted Beckett and pulled a gun.

Beckett bent Severin's arm to the side, disarming him. "On your knees. Now."

A stirring behind him caught a second of his attention. Aurora.

Severin rushed him, knocking the gun from Beckett's grasp and landing on top of him.

Beckett clamped Severin's chin and pushed him off his chest, then went for the gun.

But not to take his life. He wasn't the judge.

He didn't pronounce the sentencing. The rage he'd felt going after Parker Hill wasn't what he felt now. He didn't want revenge. He wanted true justice. And that meant taking Severin down alive if he could.

Severin dove into him as they both grappled for the weapon; Severin snatched the gun, and aimed it at Beckett.

Beckett grabbed Severin's hands, working to push the gun away from his own nose. Dirt and twigs dug into the back of his shirt.

"I will kill you!" Severin growled.

That's when he saw her stumbling his way. Dirt clinging to her body. Eyes wild. Hair matted and filthy.

She had something in her hand.

Beckett kneed Severin in the groin as Aurora brought the shovel down on his head.

He went still.

Beckett rolled him onto the grass, checked his

pulse to find it still thumping and snatched the gun as Aurora crumpled in a heap on the ground.

"Aurora!" He slid to her side, brushing her hair from her face. Whisking his jacket off the dirt pile, he covered Aurora with it. He clutched his phone and called for an ambulance and backup.

Pulling her into his lap, he kissed her dirty forehead. "Stay with me, Aurora." He rocked her back and forth, praying, pleading as they waited for first responders. "Stay with me, baby."

This woman had saved his life. In more ways than one.

He'd felt dead for so long. But Aurora had slipped into his soul and breathed life back into him. Proved he could love again. Wholly. Fiercely. She couldn't leave him. Not now. *God, thank You. Make a way for us.*

Her skin was like ice and her lips had turned a deeper shade of blue. He continued to cradle her, his back to the wind to help keep her warm. "Hang on for me. Don't leave me. Please don't leave me, Aurora."

He nuzzled his face into her neck, burying his mouth against her frigid skin as he whispered his pleas into her ear. "You're a fighter. That's what you do. Don't you give up," he demanded. "That's right. I'm telling you what to do. Makes you mad, doesn't it? Wake up and give me a fight, Aurora. Fight. For yourself. For me."

Aurora didn't move.

Beckett kissed her dried and cracked lips. "I love you."

FOURTEEN

Beckett kissed Aurora's hand and gently laid it by her side. She'd been sleeping for the last couple of hours. She was going to be okay. Back to normal.

Beckett wasn't sure he was.

He couldn't lose her. Ever.

He'd been sitting here praying about what to do. Where to go from here. He wanted everyone to be happy. Him. Aurora. Mama.

The only shot he had was to take the job in Atlanta. The distance wasn't a strong enough barrier between them anymore. He'd realized that after almost losing her. He'd make it work. If she would. And the truth was, he wanted that position. But could he hurt the woman who'd given him life to be with the woman he wanted to spend the rest of his with?

Exiting Aurora's room for a cup of coffee before she woke, he bumped into Mama. What was she doing here?

"Hey," he said, his throat dry and scratchy like his heart.

"I got here about ten minutes ago. Melody from Admitting called. Said you were here. Deputy Ferrell is outside and explained everything." She touched his shoulder, took in his grimy face. He hadn't had time to wash up. Didn't want to leave Aurora. Had phones calls to make. "I brought you some fresh clothes."

"Thank you."

"I've been watching you watch her. I haven't seen you this way in a long time. I'm not sure I've *ever* seen you this way."

Beckett wasn't so sure he'd ever been this way, either. "She's unlike anyone I've ever met."

"You mean she's not Meghan."

His chest ached. "I mean she's one of a kind. Nothing like I imagined." She'd crawled out of her grave to rescue him.

"Then why so many worry lines on that forehead? I heard she's going to be okay."

"She is. It's complicated, Mama."

"Life is complicated, baby. But without the complications, you wouldn't have the exhilarating joy when it's not. You wouldn't appreciate the simple things—like a stroll through the park or the way a hug from someone you love touches all the way to your toes. You wouldn't admire the beauty of a butterfly or a belly laugh with an old friend. We need complicated."

"I like the way you see things. But I could stand a break from complication for a while." Sometimes he could hardly catch his breath before another dilemma arose.

"The Good Lord gives us complications to teach us dependence on Him. To teach us to trust a little longer, to walk in faith a little farther, to live a little louder."

How true that statement was. He'd had to depend on God to find Aurora, to save Aurora. He wasn't a savior. Judge. He was a man who needed help from the One who was Savior. Judge. Always. "I love you, you know that?" Beckett draped his arm around her. "You've been the constant in my life, sacrificing for me and letting me go into the navy with your blessing, but I know it was hard on you. I know you—"

"Go." The command knocked him for a little loop.

"What? Where?" He glanced at the change of clothes she'd brought him.

Leaning into him, she curled her arm around his bicep. "Go to Atlanta, Beck. I've missed the dance in your eyes. At first I thought it was grief over Meghan. Then I realized it was more than that—when I was positive you'd moved on emotionally from her. I knew it was the job here."

He swallowed hard.

"I should have piped up then, but I was selfish. I wanted you here, safe and where I could see you or hear your voice whenever I wanted. Turns out you're not truly safe anywhere. These past few weeks have shown me that."

"Mama," he choked, "you are the least selfish person I know."

She squeezed his upper arm and sniffed. "I know you've dodged Wilder's calls. He's made several to me. But then he showed up. That boy has tenacity." She shook her head, garnering a laugh from them both.

"I want to take care of you. Be here for you like you've been for me. I don't want you to worry about me."

Mama slipped from his reach and cupped his cheeks. "You are my baby. I don't care if you're six foot three. I don't care if you know how to get in and out of countries with no one knowing. I don't care that you're thirty-two years old. I will worry about you if you farm potatoes or launch nuclear weapons. I want you to be happy."

Beckett's breath hitched. "I thought you were glad to have me here. In less danger. Safe."

"Well, of course I am! I'd like to put you in a bubble and never let you out of my living room. Especially after this fiasco!" She laughed through a few tears. "She makes you happy, Beckett.

Working with Wilder all over the world would make you happy. And I know the obstacles that you'd face here with Aurora. Small town. But in Atlanta…"

"Would you come to Atlanta?" He wanted to take care of her. To take care of Aurora.

"No. My life is here. I'm sixty-five years old. You've barely even started living, son. If what's holding you back from her is sticking around to make your old mama happy, then buck up, kiddo. I'm on board with you leaving."

"But the assignments…"

"Can be dangerous. I get it. But God made you who you are, Beckett Levi Marsh. Not everyone can do the kinds of things you've done. You rescued dozens of people from a building that exploded. You dug a woman from a grave with your bare hands and took down the monster who put her there. He gave you the moxie to do it. Now muster up some of it to tell your mama what you really want and that you're moving."

Beckett's chest tightened. "You're the best thing ever, Mama." He hugged her and kissed the top of her head. "I want Aurora, and if I have to move across the world to make her mine, then I'll do it."

"Well, I said Georgia, not across the world." She leaned into his embrace. "Make her yours. Providing she feels the same way. She ain't one to be bossed."

"No, she's not." But would she want to move to Georgia at some point? What would it take to practice law there? He wouldn't ask her to give up what she loved. He couldn't. Would she even see his move as a chance to be together?

"I know. I saw it that day she came over and gave you a run for your money. I like her. And I think someday I'd like a few little redheaded grandbabies to visit." She gave him a playful push. "Go on, now. You don't want her seeing you all filthy when she wakes. Clean up, then do what you know is right."

Beckett gave her one last look before hurrying to the restrooms. When Aurora woke, he'd tell her the truth. He loved her. And between the two of them and a heap of prayer, they'd find a way to spend their lives together.

Beeps and buzzing woke her.

Aurora blinked. At first the scenery was blurry, but then she gained her focus.

White walls.

Monitors.

Her body was drenched in wonderful warmth. She touched the fabric over her legs. Heated blankets.

She was in the hospital. Everything was fuzzy, but then Severin's face…the box… She'd been buried! Fresh fear filled her.

"Hey, hey," came a reticent whisper. "You're safe. I'm here. Right here."

Beckett.

Beckett had come for her.

And almost died.

She'd passed out, then awoken, and Severin had a gun. He was going to kill Beckett.

Shovel.

Her mouth felt like cotton and she licked her lips.

Beckett brought a cup to her mouth. "Drink. It's warm."

"Don't…tell me…what…to do," she croaked, but obeyed.

"That's my girl. My fighter." He kissed her forehead and took the cup away.

"How long have I been here?" Her head ached and she was exhausted.

"Several hours. You passed out from lack of oxygen inside the box and then again after, and you have a case of mild hypothermia. Gotta stick around here for at least forty-eight hours." He grasped her hand and laid his forehead against it. "You saved my life, Aurora Daniels."

"We're even then," she whispered, her throat hoarse from screaming. "What happened to Severin? How did you find me? I lost the bracelet. It fell off."

Beckett scooted his chair closer to her bed. He

smelled wonderful. Woodsy. Sweet. Like home. "He's going back to prison, and this time there won't be any escaping. Even if I have to keep tabs on him daily."

"But my bracelet."

Beckett stroked her hand with his thumb. "I did it the old-school way and with a lot of prayer. I found your bracelet. You were about a mile and a half from it."

"You sniffed it out and hunted him down. I prayed you would. Severin murdered Linda. In my house. She has the murder weapon, Beckett!" She tried to sit up, felt weak, and Beckett gently nudged her back down.

"Relax. It's all okay." He pressed his lips to her hand, kissed her knuckles. She was taken care of. Thanks to God. And Beckett. Both relentless.

"One of my deputies found an abandoned car near your house. I had him do a check. It was rented out of Memphis under Severin's mother's sister's name. The deputy did a sweep of your house. They found Linda and the weapon. It's already been sent off for testing. But I believe we'll find Gus's DNA and Linda's prints on it."

"And Darla?"

"Darla's fine, too. In a fair amount of shock, but that's understandable after hearing the truth. She never had a single clue about Linda, though she'd suspected Gus had been unfaithful throughout the years."

Aurora clutched her chest, relieved. "Linda said she was suicidal. I was afraid she'd killed her and made it appear like one. Tried to pin everything on Darla."

"She might have tried had Severin not gotten to her, instead."

"What about Oliver? Severin was going to frame him somehow."

"Oliver is alive. I made a call once we got you in here. To check. He's got a sister down in Florida and he's staying with her while he takes a leave of absence to reassess his life, his priorities. Said if you need him for anything, he'll come."

"And what did you say to that?"

He kissed her hand again. "Not to worry. You're in capable hands already."

Aurora scooted up on the bed and held a hand up to stop Beckett from laying her back down. "You know, I laid in that box," she shuddered, "and once I realized I had to conserve oxygen, I prayed and I thought. Beckett, I want to attempt to make this work. I know it'll be tough. We won't be able to discuss work, especially when it comes to arrests and my clients. I know the town will wonder if we divulge information to each other, but we can remain full of integrity. Especially you, because that's who…" She coughed and Beckett gave her a sip of warm tea again. "That's who you are."

His smile urged her on.

"I'm all about being frank."

"Say it isn't so," he teased.

"It's not the fact we've been thrown together in a tense situation. I was afraid that's what it might have been at first." She struggled to read his emotions, unsure if he was amused or surprised. "Well? Do you want to try? I'd rather risk trying and being brokenhearted than not being with you at all and always regretting it." She closed her eyes and reopened them. "I'm being too forward. I've never done this. I've never been in love before."

He went slack-jawed, then scooted closer to her, raw emotion a flurry upon his face. He caressed her cheek, her admission visibly affecting him. "I love you, too."

"You do?" She licked her bottom lip. "You love me?"

"So much it hurts." He leaned down and kissed her cheek. "I want to make it work. However, I'm moving. And before you argue, it's not only because of you or that moving is our only shot at this. It's because I want to. I feel like it's what I'm meant to do."

Aurora believed it down to her pinky toe.

"But you *are* a factor. Because I think about the

people I love. There's nothing wrong with that. It's what you're doing without realizing it."

She opened her mouth to protest, but he was right. Clamping her mouth shut, she simply nodded in agreement.

"And it *will* be too much of a strain on us if I stay," Beckett added.

"It would be." She rubbed her thumb over his callused knuckle. "You're sure this is what you want?"

"I want you, Aurora. And…I want to use my abilities in a broader scope. I've been hiding for fear I might do something horrible if emotionally entangled in a high-risk situation, but when I saw what Renzetti had done to you…what he intended for you…all I wanted was to get you safe. To see him punished, but by the law. And I knew that God had healed me and corrected my thinking. I can do this. Do it right."

"You're an amazing man, Beckett." Aurora was glad Beckett had chosen Atlanta. She wasn't exactly sure how it would all play out. She wasn't ready to up and leave yet. She had responsibilities. And it might be too soon for wedding bells, though the thought of becoming Mrs. Beckett Marsh nearly sent her over the moon. And, of course, he hadn't exactly asked her to marry him or even to come to Atlanta. "What about your mom?"

"Well, I had an interesting conversation with her."

Aurora shifted and winced. "You told her you wanted to work with Wilder?"

"She told me." He leaned in and lowered his voice. "She's kind of bossy."

"Apple doesn't fall far from the tree."

He tugged lightly at a strand of her hair. "Turns out, while she does want me safe and close, she wants my happiness more."

"She loves you. And people think about others when they love them."

"That is an awesome observation. You should kiss whoever told you that. And not on the cheek or in a friendly way, either." His husky voice sent a wild dance through her middle.

"Well, I'll certainly consider it."

"Do that."

She'd tell him not to tell her what to do, but kissing Beckett was exactly what she wanted to do. For the rest of her life.

He held her gaze several moments, longing passing through it, and then he cleared his throat to cut the heavy tension flowing between them. "Once you're released, I'm flying out to Atlanta to talk to Wilder. I want you to come with me, if you want to."

What was he saying? For good? For now? "Beckett, I'm not licensed in Georgia, and I'm not sure they practice reciprocity. I may have to take a short exam or something. And I have responsibilities here. I can't up and—"

He enveloped her hand with both of his and brought it to his lips. "I want you to come for the weekend. I have loose ends to tie up here, and I'm not asking you to move to Atlanta."

"Oh." Disappointment washed over her.

"Right now. But at some point, I'm sure I'll tell you to." A sly grin slid across his face, and he leaned down to peck her nose.

Of course he would. Asking would be out of the question. "Where in Atlanta?"

"Wilder inherited a plantation home and had a lot of remodeling done to turn it into a firm. Offices. A couple of apartments."

"You have to live there?"

Beckett laughed. "I'm not living on a plantation with Wilder. I want my own house. In the country. With a big yard to raise kiddos."

To be the mother of Beckett's children. Nothing sounded better. Other than to be his wife. "I like the way you think...most of the time."

Beckett leaned across the bed, his woodsy, sweet scent sending a million thrills through her. "I have paperwork to do," he said as he nuzzled his nose against hers. "So I'm leaving for an hour." He pressed a kiss to the corner of her mouth. "I'll bring you dinner and dessert when

I come back," he whispered, and added another kiss to the other corner.

"Of course you will," she rasped, light-headed.

He skimmed his thumb across her bottom lip and studied it ardently. "I expect you to rest while I'm gone, Counselor."

Fat chance.

"Don't tell me what—"

He cut off her remark with a kiss that sent her flying to places she'd only dreamed of going. A kiss that could never be described as friendly. He broke away, his breath ragged. "Maybe I'll be gone *less* than an hour." He gave her one more gentle kiss and left her lovesick.

When the door closed, Aurora grabbed her phone and checked into licensing in Georgia. Atlanta would be warmer. Not too far from beaches. Beckett hadn't proposed, but he'd implied a happily-ever-after for them, and that kiss had sealed the implication with a promise.

God had protected her, given her the strength to help Beckett and given her peace over her past. With Aurora's testimony, the photos and the wrench containing all the DNA evidence and prints, Richie's name would be officially cleared. It appeared God was placing her back on the path she'd wanted to take as a young girl. To be married, have a family of her own.

And with Beckett Marsh. The sheriff she'd always believed hated her. She pulled the covers up to her chin and snickered. No, this man loved her. Sacrificially.

A beautiful picture of how Jesus loved her. Fought for her. Died for her.

And she'd done nothing to deserve it.

But she'd take it. Every last drop of love and grace God wanted to pour out.

He was worth loving.

And so was Beckett.

She was ready.

FIFTEEN

April

Beckett paced his backyard. For the last eight weeks, he'd been preparing for this moment. After filling out paperwork and making sure his county had a capable sheriff in charge, he'd put his home up for sale and packed up his belongings. The worst part was leaving Aurora.

She'd healed, gained her strength, purchased a new wardrobe and helped him pack. His house had sold after one week on the market. God had His hand in all of this.

Aurora had flown out with him to meet the team and had hit it off with everyone. Wilder mentioned needing a good legal mind on the team and offered Aurora a job on the spot. Which she'd jumped on.

Over the past few weeks he'd been in Atlanta, Aurora had flown down and helped him house hunt. Her favorite had been the updated modern farmhouse with ten acres of land less than thirty minutes—if the traffic was good—from the firm. The minute she flew back to Hope, he'd put an offer on it. As far as she knew, he was still hunting for the right place while living in the guest house at Wilder's plantation, and she'd been searching online for condos. As if he'd ever let her live apart from him once she made the move.

Would she be surprised? Would she think he was ridiculous? He was. He didn't care. One last check of his watch and it was time to pick her up at the airport.

He met her at the baggage claim, where she ran into his arms and he peppered her with kisses. "I missed you."

"I missed you, too. But I'm glad we get to spend Easter weekend together. I tried to talk your mom into flying out with me, but she said she had things to take care of and would fly in Saturday."

Beckett refrained from commenting. Mama was in on this, too. He rolled her luggage to the parking garage.

"You pick a house yet?"

"I did."

"Beckett," she shrieked, and beamed. "Why didn't you tell me? Which one?"

"I'm surprising you." They made small talk, mostly Beckett deflecting Aurora's questions about the house. He enveloped her hand and exited the interstate.

She studied her surroundings. "I know where we are, Beckett Marsh. You picked the farmhouse."

He drove down the long drive and up to the house with a large wraparound porch. Pastureland on either side. A large backyard. "I did. Come on. I want to show you something."

"You dirty dog." She giggled as he laced his hand in hers and headed toward the backyard. "What? I've seen everything."

"Have you?"

"What have— What is that?" She made a puzzled face, then lit up. "Is that what I think it is?"

He tugged her along in a jog and waited while she took it all in, staring in what appeared to be complete awe. He pulled a pink plastic egg from his shirt pocket, his nerves in a frenzy.

"You have chickens!" She threw back her head and laughed.

No, *they* had chickens. "I want you to be able to have your courage every single day. That morning when you told me why you ate eggs, I think that was the moment I fell in love with you. It was definitely the moment I knew there was more to you than meets the eye."

Aurora stared at the chicken coop, hens and a rooster milling about.

When she turned back, he dropped to his knee and held out the plastic egg. She snickered. "Those are some eggs the hens lay."

"Aurora Millicent Daniels. I love you. I can't imagine my life without you. Marry me." He handed her the egg, and she opened it and gasped. He guessed he'd done well.

"It's oval. Like an egg!" She peered down at him, eyes pooling.

"It'll take bravery to be married to me." He stood, hoping she'd realize there was some truth to that teasing statement.

"So that's why you *really* bought all the chickens. Endless supply of eggs." She laughed again. He'd never tire of hearing it.

"Possibly. Say yes."

She chewed her bottom lip, a mischievous glint in her eyes. "Don't tell me what to do." Rising on her tiptoes, she kissed his chin.

The rooster crowed. Chickens squawked. He hadn't asked. Not exactly. "Aurora, would you be my wife? Would you let me love you the rest of my life?"

"Yes. Yes, I will. If you let me love you the rest of mine."

He placed the sparkling oval diamond with a halo of surrounding diamonds on her left ring finger, then he pulled her to him, loving the way she fit perfectly against him.

His lips met hers, sending wildfire through his blood, but he held it back yielding to a slow, lingering kiss, lavished in loyalty, devotion and a promise to cherish her always and forever.

She broke away. "Did you ever once think you'd marry a defense attorney?"

"Certainly not. But I'm proud to call you my wife, Aurora. What you did for Richie? You risked everything. The whole world knows he was always innocent. He'd be so proud of you, too. I know it."

He wiped a tear from her eye. "I think we should put a pool over there." He pointed across the way. "Kids like pools. And since we're having four of them..." he teased.

"There you go again telling me what I'm gonna do." She leaned into him as they walked toward the house. "I'm going to break you of those commanding ways. I promise you that."

"One for each of our hands makes sense."

"That's what you're bringing to the table? One for each hand?"

He kissed the top of her head. "It's just the beginning of my opening statement, Counselor." He'd never stop loving these little arguments. Or Aurora Daniels—soon to be Marsh.

Not ever.

* * * * *

Dear Reader,

Admittedly, I struggled with Aurora Daniels and her profession (at first). Something similar happened in my life when a drunk teenager hit my brother-in-law and killed him. That pain rippled through my family. Some have healed. Some remain bitter. I had to resolve in *my* heart that God is in control even in tragedy. In pain. In suffering. In loss. And that He's forgiving. Not to some. But to all who ask. When unfair things happen in our lives, we have to trust that God will sort out the injustice. If not here, in eternity. I pray that you'll ask Him to heal you, and believe that He'll do it. Always. He loves you completely.

I'd love for you to stay in the loop about book releases and inside info only those who subscribe to my newsletter, *Patched In*, receive. You can join at: www.jessicarpatch.com.

Warmly,
Jessica

Get 2 Free Books,

Plus 2 Free Gifts—

just for trying the

Reader Service!

Get 2 Free Books,
Plus 2 Free Gifts—
just for trying the Reader Service!

HARLEQUIN
HEARTWARMING™

HWI7